Other Trevc

A Case For Drones

The debut novel in the Matt Talbot series, in which Talbot, a CIA contractor and a veteran of the war against Al Qaeda in Afghanistan, helps piece together the elements of a sinister plot against the USA, the likes of which could never have been imagined. His team's task is to help thwart the plot, ultimately resulting in previously unprecedented agreements changing the face of history between superpowers.

Trevor's Travels

Stories of a world traveler in the information technology industry; his adventures, challenges, opportunities, and romances.

Both books are available in kindle and paperback formats from Amazon.

Hunters, Hackers and Hermits

Hunters, Hackers and Hermits

Trevor Dodd

A Matt Talbot Novel

Hunters, Hackers and Hermits by Trevor Dodd.

Published in kindle e-book form in 2016.

Copyright © 2016 by Trevor Dodd.

Cover illustration and design Mark Peters.

All rights reserved. No part of this book may be reproduced, scanned, or distributed in any printed or electronic form without permission. Please do not participate in or encourage piracy of copyrighted materials in violation of the author's rights. Purchase only authorized editions.

This is a work of fiction. Names, characters, places, and incidents are either the product of the author's imagination, or are used fictitiously, and any resemblance to actual persons, living or dead, business establishments, events or locales is entirely coincidental. The publisher does not have any control over and does not assume any responsibility for author or third-party Web sites or their contents.

ISBN-13: 978-1-5238-2782-4
ISBN-10: 1-5238-2782-3

10 9 8 7 6 5 4 3 2 1

Everything I write has a precedent in truth.

Ian Fleming.

Contents

Prologue:: Abbottābad..1
Chapter 1: La Jolla Farms..4
Chapter 2: Visiting the SAS...6
Chapter 3: Facial Reconstruction...14
Chapter 4: Searching for Matt Talbot.......................................16
Chapter 5: The American Embassy...22
Chapter 6: Chase through the Fens...30
Chapter 7: Relaxing with Friends..33
Chapter 8: Back in La Jolla...37
Chapter 9: The Hacker Report..44
Chapter 10: Planning the Visit to the Hermit Kingdom..........52
Chapter 11: Back to the Kimchi...55
Chapter 12: Visiting Langley..61
Chapter 13: La Jolla Again..67
Chapter 14: And More Kimchi..69
Chapter 15: Pyongyang...73
Chapter 16: Langley Again...76
Chapter 17: The White House..78
Chapter 18: The Tunnel..80
Chapter 19: The Pyongyang Dilemma.....................................85
Chapter 20: Visiting Shenyang...87
Chapter 21: Back to the Garlic Eaters......................................92
Chapter 22: Home Again..96
Chapter 23: CIA Headquarters..100
Chapter 24: Tunnel Paranoia..110
Chapter 25: 1600 Pennsylvania Avenue.................................112
Chapter 26: The Team Flies In..116
Chapter 27: The Pieces Come Together.................................120
Chapter 28: Readying the Offensive......................................122
Chapter 29: Final Preparations for the Response.................124
Chapter 30: Shock and Awe..127
Epilogue..137

Acknowledgments

I would first like to thank Arlo Nugent for his superb advice and early reviews given his firsthand knowledge of visiting North Korea, and his experience with some of the weaponry mentioned.[1] Thanks also to Mark Peters who again helped me through the process of formatting and finalizing the text, creating cover artwork, and publishing.[2] My sincere thanks to Jenny Blunt, a dear friend for the last forty plus years, who reminded me of accident black spots in the fens of Norfolk, and repaired my memory of some of the best dining venues surrounding my home town in the UK. And thanks to John Dutton who gave me a few tips about my description of the Caterham 7. As always, thanks to Martha Smith for her encouragement and generosity in taking the time to review my early drafts, and my thanks also to Candy Tyner and Bob Prendergast for their continuing encouragement.

Much research was needed to fill gaps in my knowledge of some countries, technologies, government organizations and other subjects. I made extensive use of Wikipedia (and other websites that it pointed me to) and wish to extend my thanks to its team for the superb service they provide.[3] Other valuable sources for research into North Korea and the SAS included The New York Times, Business Insider, CNN, The Guardian, Daily Mail and Fox News. And lastly, kudos to Apple, Inc. for the iPad Air, the iPad Pro and the Pages application, my primary tools for the creation of this book.

---

1   www.bluechipsd.com
2   www.litera.com.au
3   www.wikipedia.org

Foreword

The description of the visits to North Korea are factual, based on an interview with a friend who traveled by coach from Seoul to Pyongyang, and research into current tourist visits to Pyongyang by air from Beijing, arranged by Koryo Tours.[4]

Descriptions of residences of Kim Jong-un and his lifestyle are in the public domain, as are accounts of famines and suffering of the general population, including malnutrition, resulting from diversions of limited funds to fulfill military and nuclear ambitions, exacerbated by punitive UN sanctions.

All accounts of visits to Seoul and the food and beverages are based on personal experience. Descriptions of the Seoul subway network are also factual, but liberties were taken regarding the links from the subway to the US Military presence in the city.

Descriptions of the SAS selection and training processes are all factual, as is the description of the underground facility built close to Hereford in the UK. The Plough Inn in Hereford exists, but its use as a 'local' by off-duty SAS personnel is a matter of conjecture.

Accounts of the journey and visits to Hereford, Norfolk and London in the UK are based on personal experience.

The tunnels from North Korea to the South are factual, other than the fifth one described in the book, but who really knows? Three of the four tunnels described in the book are open to visiting tourists traveling to South Korea, but they have been since been rendered unusable as a means of crossing the DMZ.

The descriptions of Russian armaments are factual.

The accounts of sarin gas and its horrific effects are factual, as is the account of Syria's illegal use of the toxin.

North Korea's extensive use of hackers based mostly in Shenyang in northeast China is factual, as is the history of the expansive and expensive efforts on such activities over recent times.

---

4   www.koryogroup.com

The accounts of restrictions in North Korea regarding Internet access and cellphone technology are also factual.

Accounts of North Korea's missile and nuclear tests up to and including the claimed hydrogen bomb test in January of 2016 are factual.

Descriptions of the heavily polluted environment in Shenyang are factual, given its reliance on heavy industry and coal mining. The smog created is appalling, especially during winter months when coal-burning plants are used to provide heating to the city. Shenyang is the biggest environmental disaster in all of China, if not the world.

The X-37B shuttles are built by Boeing Phantom Works for the US Air Force. They have conducted several unmanned long-term missions over recent years with no public disclosure as to their purpose.

Mentions of sanctions and military operations enacted prior to and including 2015 are factual, as are references to US military armaments.

Descriptions of the North Korean navy and its strength, capabilities and bases vary; a summary of reports is presented here.

Hotels and other hostelries mentioned in the book all exist.

Principal Characters

Matt Talbot, CIA contractor
Al-Kuwaiti, Al Qaeda, who morphed into Hassan
Shagufta, Al Qaeda sympathizer
Al-Zarian, killed during the Abbottābad raid
Humam, new head of Pakistan Al-Qaeda cell
Wuhayshi, Al-Qaeda/CIA double-agent
Federica Ferrari, Matt's new girlfriend
Captain Brian Philips, SDPD
Major Mark Smyth, SAS (retired)
Todd Miller, Director, CIA Clandestine Services
Dieter Bleschmidt, CIA agent, Zürich
Peter Ellis, Al-Qaeda sleeper agent, London
Salman, Ellis' friend at Eton and Oxford
Roland St. John Finch, ex-SAS
Jeff Herd, Al-Qaeda sleeper agent, San Diego
Pete Scott, Metropolitan Police, London
Steve Marcella, CIA agent, London
Cedric Jackson, MI6
Colonel Joe Howard, US Army, Itaewon, Seoul
BM Min, tunnel project, Pyongyang
JW Hyung, Chairman, South Korean offensives, Pyongyang
KC Park, responsible for Itaewon mole, Pyongyang
John Peel, Director, CIA, Langley
William Mitchell, Secretary of State, White House
Melissa Osborne, National Security Advisor, White House
Hillary Clinton, President of the United States
General Bertrand Rushmore, Chairman of the Joint Chiefs of Staff
Park Geun-hye, President of South Korea
Jack Mathis, Director, CIA Seoul
Dr. March, CDC, Atlanta
Marty Lee, tunnel expert, Seoul
KS Mac, sarin gas expert, Pyongyang
HS Kim, sarin gas expert II, Pyongyang

CS Lee, CIA agent, Shenyang
Choe, GM, Cybertek satellite office, Shenyang
Jeong, GM, Cybertek main office, Shenyang
Dirk Potter, Director, CIA Seoul, replacing Jack Mathis
Nick Bailey, CIA armorer
Dr. Black, Langley's 'Q'
Bill Patrick, Secretary of Defense
Admiral George Pennington, Coalition Navy Force

Matt's team: Mark Smyth, Peter Brennan, Ganju (Ganja) Lama, Bhanbhagta (Bang Bang) Gurung and Lloyd Morris

Prologue: Abbottābad

Pakistan, 2017

EARLIER IN 2017 MATT TALBOT had led his team in an attack on the underground complex housing Al Qaeda leaders in Abbottābad, Pakistan. It had been the culmination of a massive effort by the CIA to thwart Al Qaeda's attempt to provoke a war between Iran and the US. The threat had already been eliminated when Talbot's team went into action, but their job was not only to destroy the bunker and its contents but also eliminate all members of the Al-Qaeda team. Unbeknown to Matt and his team, Al-Kuwaiti, one of the terrorists, had somehow survived the explosive blasts after Talbot's team left, by taking shelter in one of the damaged tunnels. He had crawled toward the main entrance, pausing frequently. He was weak, suffering from severe blood loss and excruciating pain from his bullet wounds. When he finally emerged from the tunnel and entered the safe house, he passed out on the floor just as the woman who lived there was returning. Shagufta cried out when she saw his condition. There was blood everywhere and it looked as if one side of his face had been gouged by shrapnel. She quickly tried to call for help but the phones had been taken out during the attack, so she patched up Al-Kuwaiti as best she could then ran to the next village to call a local doctor known to be sympathetic to their cause. After listening to Shagufta's description of the wounds, he packed his bag and drove them both back to where Al-Kuwaiti was laying. He praised Shagufta's efforts to staunch the flow of blood that had unquestionably saved his life and set to work, removing bullets and shrapnel before stitching him up. He gave Shagufta a supply of painkillers and antibiotics before promising to come back and visit in a few days. She slowly nursed Al-Kuwaiti back to health, gradually weaning him away from a liquid diet until he could eat soft foods, and she found a dentist who could remedy the damage to his teeth and gums. His once handsome face was now terribly scarred though his body finally started functioning properly after a few months. During his recovery, Al-Kuwaiti began having recollections of what had transpired during the bunker firefight. In flashes of light caused by the stun grenades and flash-bangs, despite the power cut, he had caught sight of the man who seemed to be the leader when he shot and killed Al-Zarian. He had heard other team members refer to this man as 'Major' and he also recalled that the 'Major' spoke with a British accent. When he felt sure of his recollections, Al-Kuwaiti called Humam, the newly appointed head of the local Al Qaeda cell, and requested a meeting. A Land Rover was sent to collect him, but not before he thanked Shagufta profusely, promising to return.

Al-Kuwaiti had a meeting with Humam and his sidekick Wuhayshi in a safe house on the outskirts of Islamabad, about seventy miles away. They embraced though Humam recoiled at the sight of his colleague's facial disfigurement. After relating his story, Al-Kuwaiti explained the reason for requesting the meeting, to ask for funding and resources to hunt down the 'Major' and bring him to justice. They talked at length and it was quickly evident that Al-Kuwaiti was determined and itching for retribution.

Humam cautioned him about impetuous behavior, then said, "first thing you need to do is undergo plastic surgery on your face. I know of a superb clinic in Switzerland. You will need a new passport. We will fund all of this given what you have been through and your knowledge of the head mercenary."

Wuhayshi photographed Al-Kuwaiti's face and promised to take care of the passport details and the trip to Switzerland.

What neither of them knew was that Wuhayshi was also a double-agent for the CIA. He was fast to contact his local field agent and pass on what he had learnt using his secure iPhone, including the photograph. Within hours the report was in the hands of Todd Miller, who had been Talbot's operations manager during the Abbottābad operation. Todd called Matt and told him to check his email while he waited.

"Good God," gasped Talbot. "Who in the world is that? If my dog was that ugly, I'd shave his ass and teach him to walk backwards."

Todd could not help chuckling but said, "That ugly bastard is a guy you thought you had killed in the bunker, but you didn't. He will probably soon have a license to hunt you down. The other news is that he's traveling to Switzerland for some serious plastic surgery so after that he'll probably look a bit more acceptable. He's starting from scratch, though. All he seems to know right now is that you are probably English and you either are or were a major."

"Well thanks, Todd. I'll keep my eyes and ears open."

"We'll be doing the same, Matt," said Todd. "And we're trying to get someone inside the clinic he'll be visiting for treatment."

The next day, a further meeting was convened among Al-Kuwaiti, Humam and Wuhayshi, and Humam announced his decision that Al Qaeda would fund the manhunt and logistical support but frequent progress reports from Al-Kuwaiti would be needed since this would probably be an extended, expensive operation. Wuhayshi announced that he had contacted Laclinic in Montreux, close to Geneva, and made an appointment for reconstructive surgery for Al-Kuwaiti. He would need a few weeks to recover after his operation.

Chapter 1
La Jolla Farms

California, 2017

MATT STILL DROVE his Aston Martin Vanquish and a Bentley Continental GT, but after the death of his ex-girlfriend Jessica, he had sold her Mercedes-AMG GT Coupe. It had brought back too many memories. Matt also owned a crappy-looking Ford F150 pickup truck, albeit in perfect mechanical condition. He used it when the occasions arose. Matt's girlfriend, Federica, owned a Lotus Evora 400, an exotic supercharged car built in Norfolk, England.[5] Matt took an immediate liking to the car, especially since owning a Caterham 7 620 R while serving with the SAS in the UK.[6] The 7 620 R was a wolf in wolf's clothing, with a two-liter supercharged Ford Duratec power plant, capable of propelling the beast to 60 mph in a sphincter-tightening 2.79 seconds. Caterham had acquired the rights from Lotus after they stopped production of the Lotus 7, the manufacturer's first road car. Talbot had a special affection for all things Lotus after visiting their plant in Hethel in his youth. Federica actually lusted after LaFerrari, given her family name of Ferrari, but her aspirations were not yet matched by her bank balance.

Federica, since experiencing Matt's culinary skills firsthand on a few occasions, was becoming an accomplished cook. She was preparing to fly to Europe for another modeling assignment and created what she hoped would be a delicious dinner for them on

---

[5] www.lotuscars.com
[6] www.caterhamcars.com

the eve of her departure. The meal started with a small salad with truffle-infused vinaigrette, followed by lobster risotto. She followed that with rack of lamb with artichokes, lemon forte, zucchinis and piment d'argile. Matt supplied the wine. He thought he was falling in love again. They retired early that night and when dawn broke he drove Federica to Lindbergh airport to catch her flight.

Talbot was at a loss after Federica left, spending much of his time with local friends. But he maintained his daily regimen in his home gym, and at least twice each week he drove to the American Shooting Center on Ruffin Road or out to the desert to hone his skills with his Kimber handgun, his Barrett sniper rifle and M4A1 carbine. He was running short of ammunition and visited his local gun shop again, who placed another bulk-buy order on his supplier in South Korea.

He also amassed several speeding tickets taking out Federica's Lotus on local roads, and invited his old friend Captain Brian Phillips of the SDPD over one evening. After a few drinks, Matt broached the subject of his tickets. Phillips sighed and agreed to make them disappear but gave Talbot a friendly warning not to ask that favor again!

Chapter 2
Visiting the SAS

Hereford, UK, 2017

THE NEXT DAY MATT was enjoying a modest breakfast and had just commanded Siri to find the BBC news on his Apple TV, when he received a call from a close friend from his SAS days. Major Mark Smyth was retiring from the regiment and had called to invite Talbot to his farewell party in Hereford. Matt jumped at the chance and accepted his offer immediately, including the invitation to stay at Mark's house while he was over there. After finishing his meal Talbot also contacted a few other old friends, in Norfolk, who he planned to visit after Hereford. He called Federica about his plans hoping they would be able to meet while he was in the UK, since she was now in Paris.

The invitation brought memories flooding back from his days commanding one of four SAS squadrons of sixty men in his rank as major. Squadrons are typically divided into four troops, each troop being commanded by a captain. Troops usually consist of fifteen men, and each patrol within a troop consists of four men, with each man having a particular skill: signals, demolition, medic or linguist besides basic skills learned during his training. The four troops specialize in four different areas: Boat troop – are specialists in maritime skills using scuba diving, kayaks and rigid-hulled inflatable boats and often train with the Special Boat Service; Air troop – are experts in free-fall parachuting, High Altitude – Low Opening (HALO) and High Altitude – High Opening (HAHO) techniques; Mobility troop – are specialists in using vehicles and are experts in desert warfare – they are also trained in an advanced level of motor mechanics to handle field-repair and vehicular breakdown; Mountain troop – are specialists in Arctic combat and survival, using specialist equipment such as skis, snowshoes and mountain-climbing techniques.

The Special Air Service is under the operational command of the Director Special Forces (DSF), a major general grade post. The UKSF originally consisted of the regular and reserve units of the SAS and the Special Boat Service, but was later joined by two new units: the Special Forces Support Group and the Special Reconnaissance Regiment. They are supported by the Signal Regiment and the Joint Special Forces Aviation Wing, part of which is based in Hereford with the SAS. In 2014 the SAS Reserve units came under the operational command of 1st Intelligence, Surveillance and Reconnaissance Brigade.

SAS selections are held twice yearly, in summer and winter, in Sennybridge in the Brecon Beacons. Selection lasts for five weeks and normally starts with about two hundred potential candidates. On arrival candidates first undergo fitness tests, and then march cross-country against the clock, increasing the distances covered each day, culminating in what is known as Endurance: a forty-mile march with full equipment scaling and descending Pen y Fan in twenty hours. By the end of the hill phase candidates must be able run four miles in thirty minutes and swim two miles in ninety minutes.

Following the hill phase is the jungle phase, taking place in Belize, Brunei, or Malaysia. Candidates are taught navigation, patrol formation and movement, and jungle survival skills. Candidates returning to Hereford finish training in battle plans and foreign weapons and take part in combat survival exercises, the final one being the week-long escape and evasion. Candidates are formed into patrols and, carrying nothing more than a tin can filled with survival equipment, are dressed in old WWII uniforms and told to head for a point by first light. The final selection test is arguably the most grueling: resistance to interrogation, lasting for thirty-six hours.

Typically, 15-20% of candidates make it through the hill phase selection process. From the approximately 200 candidates, most will drop out within the first few days, and by the end about thirty will remain. Those who do are rewarded with a transfer to an operational squadron.

Talbot shuddered as he recalled his participation in these selection torture tests, but he had fared well and quickly rose to the rank of major, subsequently talking part in raids during the Gulf War of 1991 before retiring. He had been chartered to lead an eight-man patrol to destroy communication links between Baghdad and northwest Iraq, and with tracking Scud missile movements in the region. Their mission had been compromised and they were forced to attempt an escape on foot toward Syria where they were rescued by helicopter, but not before one of Talbot's men died of heat exhaustion.

Putting such memories behind him again, Matt began planning his trip. The most convenient way to reach the UK was to fly in his airplane to LAX, so he fired up the Aston and drove to Montgomery Field (known as KMYF to pilots). Montgomery Field is six miles north of downtown San Diego, and is one the nation's busiest airports for small aircraft and has several flying clubs, flight schools, plus business turboprops and jets based there, including Matt's airplane. His pilot and copilot had already filed a flight plan, and had had the Bombardier Learjet 85 fueled and loaded with food and drinks. His Learjet was the latest generation of an aircraft positioned between the midsize and super-midsize segments. It could comfortably seat eight passengers in addition to the two pilots, could cruise at Mach 0.80 at an altitude of forty-one thousand feet or higher if necessary, and had a range of three thousand nautical miles. In addition to the state-of-the-art avionics that came as standard, Matt had installed entertainment systems, and Wi-Fi and cellphone connectivity such that his Apple iToys were always operable, having contracted with OnAir out of Switzerland for their Internet, Mobile and Link OnAir services. Since Apple had announced 4K video support for its Apple TV, Talbot had upgraded his on-board display to enjoy the latest content available. Matt had a license to fly the Learjet but after logging the necessary hours to keep it current, he usually just relaxed as a passenger.

From LAX he took a British Airways flight to London. He had not flown with them since they had revamped their first-class cabin and was looking forward to experiencing their new service. He was not disappointed. As usual they served drinks before take-off and Matt was reminded of an announcement made famous several years ago when a flight attendant pronounced, "we need to collect your glasses now but you can hold onto your nuts." So Matt held onto his nuts and after takeoff checked email on his iPad, but found nothing of consequence except a sweet note from Federica and a brief message from Todd Miller, Director of Clandestine Services for the CIA, to call when he reached London. The meal service began and after canapés and other delights he enjoyed a delicious dinner of breast of corn-fed chicken with English summer truffle and tarragon sauce, samphire, wild mushrooms and baby carrots, followed by a cheese plate that included two of his favorites, Stilton and farmhouse cheddar. He ordered a Cockburn's Fine Tawny Port with his coffee and started to watch a movie before drifting off to sleep. He awoke to be served with a very civilized full English breakfast, the highlights of which were back bacon, pork sausage, grilled tomatoes, mushrooms and scrambled eggs, before landing in Heathrow. The traditional baked beans were missing but Matt understood BA's reluctance to serve flatulence-inducing delights!

Major Smyth was there to meet him when he cleared customs, and they began the drive to Hereford in the Caterham 7 that Matt had sold to him when he retired from the SAS. More memories of the UK flooded back as they walked to the car through torrential rain. Fortunately Smyth had already erected the soft-top, such as it was. Matt somehow squeezed into his seat after cramming in his luggage given the absence of a boot. He was pleased he always traveled lightly. But otherwise he thoroughly enjoyed the drive despite the lack of creature comforts, until they made a brief stop and he returned Todd's call on his iPhone.

"Hi Matt," said Todd when they finally connected. "Thanks for calling. I realize you're on vacation."

"So what's new?" asked Matt.

"Well, Wendy and I are expecting a baby!" said Todd, sounding very pleased with himself.

"You mean Wendy, your wife?" asked Matt.

"Asshole," quipped Todd.

"You mean you've manufactured a little shitting machine at your age?" asked Matt.

"Double asshole," said Todd, laughing. "But that's not the reason I wanted to talk. We're hearing whispers about something serious going down and probably need your talents again. How long will you be in Hereford and could you come to London afterward?"

"Nothing firm in Hereford, but most likely about ten days. I'm driving to Norfolk after that but could postpone my visit. What's going on in London?" asked Matt.

"I can fly over and meet you at the embassy on Grosvenor Square where we can talk. Don't want to say much more now because I'm not sure how secure these roaming calls are."

"OK sure," replied Matt. "I can change my schedule and email you the details."

"Thanks, Matt. I usually stay at the Marriott, just a short walk from the embassy in Mayfair. I can book you a room there."

"A suite," said Matt, "I'll ask Federica whether she can fly in from Paris."

"OK, Matt," groaned Todd, "but go easy on the expenses."

"Always a pleasure talking to you," said Matt, and cut the call.

After all the assurances from Apple and the CIA's own testing, Todd apparently still did not trust his iPhone's security.

Soaked to the skin and grateful that his iPhone was waterproof, Talbot rejoined Smyth in the car and told him he had to travel to London for a few days after Hereford and left it at that. They took the M4 and the M50 and just relaxed and caught up for the rest of the day when they reached Smyth's home after only two hours. The journey had been about 130 miles but the Caterham had just eaten them up, despite the weather.

One of the most intriguing parts of Matt's visit was when Smyth took him on a tour of the recently completed underground training facility, dug into a hillside at Pontrilas Army Training Area (PATA) in rural Herefordshire close to the SAS HQ.

"Money was no object," Smyth explained. "We were given everything we asked for."

Reputed to have cost around £100M, the bunker is equipped with, among other things, kill rooms built to mimic the buildings crack teams may one day have to fight in. The site has a two-hundred yard firing range and walls covered with rubber insulation to reduce the sound of gunfire and explosions. Notably, the state-of-the-art bunker houses a Boeing 747 where soldiers can practice how to deal with incidents should terrorists capture planes and hold dozens of hostages for ransom, and the facility can house additional jumbo jets that may be deemed necessary. Approval for the new structure was forthcoming in the wake of recent attacks in Paris, to enhance readiness for the Al Qaeda threat and, following complaints from local residents, to cut the noise currently caused by explosions and constant rifle fire during exercises. Since it is underground, it is not visible from the air or satellite surveillance. SAS helicopters on training missions also changed their routes to further improve noise abatement in nearby residential areas.

The leaving party took place in The Plough Inn on Whitecross Road in Hereford, a pub often frequented by off-duty SAS personnel. A typically British establishment, it offers superb pub grub besides all manner of libations. It was a long evening and a coach had been arranged to take most of them home afterward; a fortuitous precaution! Mark Smyth had his driver on call when it was time for him and Matt to leave. About forty men showed up, almost everyone under Major Smyth's command, other than those deployed elsewhere. Most of the men had already eaten, but Smyth and Talbot had not and they chose mixed grill from the menu. It was a while since Matt had enjoyed such a meal, and was soon confronted with sirloin steak, lamb chop, lambs liver, pork sausage, the ubiquitous baked beans and chunky, soggy chips. They both loved it. Talbot asked Smyth what his future plans were, but Smyth had not really thought it through, other than wanting to retire at the pinnacle of his career, while he was alive. When they sneaked out for a cigar Talbot asked his friend whether he might be interested in clandestine work should the occasion arise and Smyth was all ears.

"The first thing I need to do though, Matt, is to try and pull my personal life together, having suffered through a bitter divorce because of my service. I've lost a few friends over the years and now is the time to try to repair some of those relationships."

"I understand completely," said Matt, "but let's stay in touch after I get back to the US."

They left it at that for now, and rejoined the festivities.

After about one hour, Smyth gave the obligatory speech and thanked all present for their service and introduced Talbot to those who had not already met him. The major was presented with a magnificent Purdey side-by-side 12-bore shotgun to add to his collection.[7] It was beautifully engraved to the specifications of the original owner. Smyth felt humbled; it must have cost a small fortune. He could hardly wait to take it out on a shoot.

Another hour passed and Smyth told Talbot he wanted to leave. After shaking the hand of every man there, he summoned his driver and they made their way home in the Land Rover. Smyth felt rather emotional but cheered up after they downed a few scotches. He even offered Matt the use of his car for the trip to London and Norfolk.

The next day Matt called Federica first about his short trip to London. She couldn't make it over there the day he arrived but could join him the day after. That actually worked out rather well, since he could meet Todd on the first day then spend a day with Federica when she arrived. He called his friends in Norfolk about his minor schedule changes, emailed the dates to Todd, and joined Smyth for a ploughman's lunch and a couple of beers in his local pub. Matt asked if he could drive the Caterham back and out of curiosity checked to see whether the switch he had installed in the

---

7   www.purdey.com; king of English gunmakers.

car was still there. The switch overrode the brake lights, either making them inoperable or turning them on when not braking, confusing the crap out of anyone who might be following.

Chapter 3
Facial Reconstruction

Switzerland, 2017

AL-KUWAITI HAD MADE slow but painful progress during his facial reconstruction at Laclinic in Montreux. He had undergone four difficult surgical procedures, and in a few days his bandages from the final operation would be removed. The surgeons were rather pleased with the outcome. One large scar would remain but for the most part it had not only been the most difficult, but also the most successful operation they had ever undertaken.

Dieter Bleschmidt, an agent in the CIA Zürich office, had attended the clinic during Al-Kuwaiti's stay, ostensibly to undergo plastic surgery to restore his facial youthfulness. Quite amazing, he mused, the perks that occasionally came with his job. But the purpose of his stay was to photograph Al-Kuwaiti after the procedures were complete. It was more difficult than it sounded since Al-Kuwaiti stayed confined to his private room as much as possible. But one day Bleschmidt finally got lucky when Al-Kuwaiti, perhaps more careless after his extended confinement, took a walk in the gardens after the bandages came off. Pretending to take photographs of the beautiful scenery, Bleschmidt managed to get several pictures of his quarry from different angles using his iPhone without detection and when he returned to his room, emailed them to his minder who forwarded them to Todd Miller.

The puzzle was coming together for Miller. He heard from Wuhayshi that Al-Kuwaiti was getting ready to leave the clinic with a new passport and identity. Chosen by Al-Kuwaiti himself, his name would now be Hassan, meaning beautiful and handsome. They made a fine pair, thought Miller; Humam, meaning brave, noble and courageous, and now Hassan. Arrogant pricks!

Chapter 4
Searching for Matt Talbot

UK and beyond, 2017

HUMAM AND HIS TEAM were working on the possible identity of the suspected British mercenary. From his behavior and probable designation of 'major' the obvious place to start looking was past and present British Army personnel. They had only a description; no photographs. The target was obviously a cut above the norm, perhaps the notorious SAS. That presented more of a challenge since the identities of these guys were heavily guarded secrets. They needed someone who could hack into the SAS databases to further their search.

Humam himself recalled a piece he had read about an ex-SAS guy who had fallen from grace after writing a book about his experiences while a member of the SAS during Desert Storm. He was persona non grata and had almost ended up in prison. Rumor had it that the guy, whose name Humam could not recall, had a serious grudge against the British military and the SAS in particular. Humam asked Wuhayshi to contact their man in the UK to learn more. Wuhayshi, of course, communicated this development to his CIA friends.

Peter Ellis had grown up in Mayfair, son of a wealthy banker. He enjoyed a privileged upbringing, first attending Eton College, then graduating from Oxford University with a Masters in Business Administration. While at Eton, he had befriended Salman from Saudi

Arabia who had also moved on to Oxford. When Salman felt comfortable confiding in Peter he talked at great length about his beliefs and the Muslim faith, eventually sharing his disdain of Christianity and all that it stood for. He persuaded Peter to travel to Saudi with him for a few months after graduation. Peter's father was furious but backed off when Peter assured him that he would seek employment in the City of London on his return.

While in Saudi, Peter was introduced to a couple of guys who turned out to be members of Al-Qaeda, as was Salman. Peter secretly converted to the Muslim faith and was recruited as a sleeper agent before returning to London. With his father's help and influence, Peter was hired into a senior post in Jardine Lloyd Thompson, one of the largest brokerage firms in the City. His lifestyle was the envy of some, living in a beautiful flat, one of many owned by his father, driving a Mercedes SL, and in the company of a seemingly endless stream of brain-dead beauties, the way he liked them. But he had never been so bored and longed for excitement. Every evening when he returned to his flat he checked the iPhone he kept stashed away. It had been given to him when he left Saudi Arabia, and he had been instructed to check for messages frequently.

On one memorable evening, he visited a local pub after work with a few of his boring colleagues, downed a few gin and tonics and returned home for an early night. He checked the phone and to his surprise found a message from Humam, asking him to call urgently. Finally, his help was needed. He was asked to track down the out-of-favor ex-SAS guy, Roland St. John Finch, to see if he could help in locating the mysterious 'major.' Finally, thought Peter, he could do something meaningful, and he experienced an unfamiliar feeling of excitement. The next day he called in sick and got to work. Finch was ridiculously easy to find. He was living in London, employed as a security guard, and was in the telephone directory. They agreed to meet and Peter explained his challenge without giving further details. Finch was not exactly a wealthy man, and demanded a fee of £5,000 up-front and a further £5,000 when he produced results. Peter had already been authorized to approve such expenditures and they parted on a handshake.

A week passed and Peter had heard nothing, and was beginning to think he had been taken for a ride, when he received a call from the elusive Finch. He had made a list, he said, of possible persons of interest.

"I took lots of risks finding these names," said Finch. "I was damned near caught."

"My price for delivery has gone up to £10,000."

"Fuck you," replied Ellis, "we had an agreement."

"Take it or leave it," retorted Finch, "Your need is greater than mine."

Ellis didn't believe that for a minute; he was bluffing; he was broke. But he offered Finch £7,500 and they had a deal. They agreed to meet and Finch handed over four names of recently retired SAS majors.

Peter took the list home with him and started making calls. He quickly crossed two of the four men off the list. One owned a pub and never went anywhere other than his own bar. Another had been killed in a traffic accident. The two remaining names were Matt Talbot, who had inherited money from his father and lived in luxury close to San Diego in California, and Trevor Wilkins, a mercenary for hire who spent most of his time in trouble spots such as Syria. Of the two, he focused most of his time on Matt Talbot. It seemed he often spent periods away from his home and no one seemed to know where he went. He took occasional vacations with his girlfriend of the moment but usually disappeared alone, either in his own airplane or by a US government jet. Ellis called Finch again and asked if he could obtain a recent photograph of Talbot.

"Maybe," replied Finch, "another £20,000 if I can."

Ellis sighed but agreed. In fact, Finch already had photographs of all four men, taken just before they left the SAS. He waited a few days and called Ellis back; they met and concluded the transaction.

Peter Ellis sent the name, address and picture of Matt Talbot off to Humam as quickly as possible, with an accounting of his expenses and fee. The details were shown to Hassan who confirmed Talbot's identity; Ellis' efforts were vindicated and funds were sent his way.

Humam took immediate further action. He had a sleeper agent in San Diego and awakened him from his long period of inactivity. He explained to Jeff Herd that he wanted eyes on Matt Talbot and gave him the address in La Jolla Farms. Jeff was asked to take a few inconspicuous drives by Talbot's house to try to spot any activity. Herd did as requested and observed that no deliveries by the US Postal Service, or anyone else for that matter, were being made. He also saw that the SDPD were driving past frequently, slowing and obviously making visual checks. Talbot was evidently out of town. Next, Herd needed to see whether Talbot's Learjet was at Montgomery Field. It was probably housed in a hangar. Herd went to see his old friend The Forger and asked for a rush job. He needed an FAA inspector ID.[8] He drove to the airfield and asked for directions to the FBO's office.[9] He showed his ID and explained he was making routine checks and needed to inspect a Learjet licensed to a Mr. Matt Talbot. He was directed to the hangar and it was indeed there. He made a note of the tail number for future reference, waited a few minutes and left the airfield. If Talbot was traveling domestically, he would have taken his own airplane. It lacked the range to leave the country, ergo he had probably taken a commercial flight. In all likelihood he would have flown from either Lindbergh Field or LAX. Herd used his contacts to check departures over the last few days and came up trumps with the flight Talbot had taken to London on British Airways.

It was time to elicit help from Peter Ellis again. His intimate knowledge of the UK and the superb job he had conducted with his previous research made Ellis the perfect candidate to try to figure out Talbot's next movements. Ellis needed Finch again. Shit, more money would need to change hands. But Finch could

---

8   Federal Aviation Administration.
9   Fixed Base Operator.

discover Talbot's most probable movements while in the UK. Once again he came through, and earned more pocket money. Finch discovered that whenever Talbot made one of his rare visits to the UK he always connected with old friends in Hereford, the home of the SAS, his alumni. He also unearthed the retirement party of Major Smyth that Talbot would undoubtedly have attended. From there, Talbot would surely travel to Norfolk to reconnect with friends from his early years. Finch kept digging and earned his fee. He learned that Talbot was to borrow Major Smyth's Caterham 7 and take an interim trip to London before taking his probable route to Norfolk using the A10 instead of faster motorways. He dutifully passed all of this on to Ellis. He even discovered the registration number of the Caterham.

When contacting Humam about these latest discoveries, Ellis prefaced his communication by warning that no effort should be expended to track down Talbot while in London, not that he even knew where he was headed. Al-Kuwaiti, now Hassan, was unfamiliar with London and after all, London had the highest concentration of CCTVs anywhere on the planet.[10] That triggered another call to Ellis.

"Do you know any corruptible London police?" Humam asked him.

"We need to know where Talbot is going so we can track his journey to Norfolk when he leaves London."

"Maybe," said Ellis, "I know a guy from my school days. I need to rekindle the friendship."

"Do I need to tell you how urgent this is?" replied Humam. Ellis hung up.

Ellis called Pete Scott early next morning. They had not spoken since Eton, but Scott owed Ellis a favor. They arranged to meet for a liquid lunch. Ellis explained he needed help in tracking a car traveling to London from Hereford on the M4. Could Scott gain access to recordings from traffic cameras?

"I work in vice, Peter," explained Scott. "I have absolutely nothing to do with traffic."

---

10   Closed Circuit TVs.

"This is really important, Pete. You must know someone who can help. I know the type of car and its registration number. I just need to know when the car enters London, where it goes, and when it leaves," pleaded Ellis, "the driver, I believe, has been meeting my girlfriend secretly, and I'm very pissed off."

"I have an idea," said Scott. You'll owe me a large dinner."

"It's a deal," smiled Ellis.

Chapter 5
The American Embassy

Grosvenor Square, London, 2017

MATT TALBOT WAS NEARING the end of his short stay in Hereford and was feeling relaxed in the company of his old friend Mark. On the evening before his departure they managed to barbecue sirloin steaks out on the patio and devoured them with salad and baked potatoes, washed down with a delicious Beaujolais.

The next morning, after a brief breakfast, Matt loaded his luggage into the car ready to start the journey to London. Mark mentioned he had placed a couple of items in a bag under the passenger seat that he thought may prove useful. It was a sunny day, perfect for driving with the top down. He stopped for coffee at a service station, but before continuing his curiosity got the better of him and he looked inside Mark's bag. There he found a pair of night-vision goggles and a SIG Sauer P232 handgun with spare clips, both SAS issue.

"Very thoughtful of Mark," he thought, "let's hope I never need them."

As he got closer to the outskirts of London, unknown to him, his journey to Grosvenor Square was being tracked right to the Marriott Hotel where he handed over the car to a valet, but not before retrieving Mark's bag that he took inside with his own. He checked in, went to his suite and called Federica, then Todd Miller. Todd was expecting his call and asked him to take the short walk to the embassy, promising lunch when he arrived. Talbot reached the

Marines guarding the entrance, showed his passport and CIA pass as instructed. He was walked to the security checkpoint and metal detector, after which he was escorted to the meeting room where Todd was waiting. The room was totally impervious to eavesdropping, the only methods of communication being a secure landline and a TEMPEST-rated Apple iMac.[11] A buffet lunch had been laid out and they helped themselves and got down to business.

"There are two major topics I need to cover," opened Miller. "One concerns you personally, and the other is a situation brewing in Korea. It will take the rest of the day, then I'll take you to dinner."

"Wow! Fire away, Todd," said Matt.

"Remember what I related to you about Al-Kuwaiti, who survived your attack in Abbottābad?" asked Todd.

"How could I forget?" Matt retorted.

"Well, he's now had reconstructive surgery, changed his name to Hassan, and with help from his asshole friends has figured out who and where you are."

"Holy shit, Todd. How in the world did he do that?" asked Matt, horrified.

"We're working on it," Todd replied. "They must have some pretty well-connected agents snooping around for them. Thanks to our double-agent Wuhayshi, we're well apprised of their antics and know Hassan will be looking for you when you leave here to drive to Norfolk. We even have a photo of him. I'm AirDropping it to you now."

"And why the fuck did you not get around to telling me any of this before?" asked Matt sarcastically.

"We wanted to be sure, Matt. And when we confirmed the stories we knew there would be no threat until you leave London. We wanted you to be relaxed while you were still safe."

Matt didn't bother to reply. Todd continued, "we now know Hassan is flying to London on Swiss International Airlines from Geneva, arriving today or tomorrow. We'll have eyes on him to

---

[11] TEMPEST is an NSA specification referring to spying on information systems through leaking emanations, including radio or electrical signals, sounds and vibrations. NSA is the National Security Agency.

figure out where he goes after landing. We don't want to pick him up and create an international incident when he has so far done nothing incriminating, but we'll have our guy following him at a distance. He's very experienced and he'll be armed. As soon as I get word about his movements from Heathrow, I'll call you. Now try one of these burgers before they get cold. They're delicious!"

Not very British, thought Matt, but he was on American soil again, kind of, so he munched on one. It was indeed rather good.

Todd poured coffee into Styrofoam cups and suggested they take a short cigar break. He led the way to an outdoor courtyard and they sat and relaxed for a few minutes, just enjoying the rare appearance of sunshine. They underwent the security checks again and returned to their safe room.

Todd broached the second item on his agenda.

"We believe the North Koreans are up to their antics again. Since their fourth tunnel-digging exploit in 1990, we helped the South Koreans sink listening equipment at strategic points south of the DMZ. We placed several heavily shielded microphones at a depth of 350' and monitor them 24x7. We are convinced they are digging another tunnel, but deeper this time."

"Any idea where they're heading for?" asked Matt.

"Too early to tell," replied Todd. "Whatever the objective, it's quite a long and laborious task. Before we take any overt action, we want to figure out why they are doing this after the failures of the past."

Todd pulled up his notes on his iPad Pro so they could easily read together.

> Since November 15, 1974, the South has discovered four tunnels crossing the DMZ that had been dug by North Korea. This is indicated by the orientation of the blasting lines within each tunnel. Upon their discovery, North Korea claimed that the tunnels were for coal mining; however, no coal was ever found in the tunnels, which were dug through granite. Some of the tunnel walls had been painted black to give the appearance of anthracite.

The tunnels are believed to have been planned as a military invasion route by North Korea. Each shaft is large enough to permit the passage of an entire infantry division in one hour, though the tunnels were not wide enough for tanks or vehicles. All the tunnels ran in a north-south direction and did not have branches. Following each discovery, engineering within the tunnels had become progressively more advanced. For example, the third tunnel sloped slightly upward as it progressed southward, to prevent water stagnation. Today, visitors may visit the second, third and fourth tunnels with guided tours.

The first of the tunnels was discovered on November 20, 1974, by a South Korean Army patrol, noticing steam rising from the ground. The initial discovery was met with automatic fire from North Korean soldiers. Five days later, during a subsequent exploration of this tunnel, US Navy Commander Robert M. Ballinger and ROK Marine Corps Major Kim Hah Chul were killed in the tunnel by a North Korean explosive device. The blast also wounded five Americans and one South Korean from the United Nations Command. The tunnel, about three feet by four feet, extended more than 62 miles beyond the Military Demarcation Line (MDL) into South Korea. The tunnel was reinforced with concrete slabs and had electric power and lighting. There were weapon storage and sleeping areas. A narrow gauge railway with carts had also been deployed. Estimates based upon the tunnel's size suggest it would have allowed approximately 2,000 KPA soldiers (one regiment) to pass through it per hour.

The second tunnel was discovered on March 19, 1975. It was of similar length to the first, located between 160 and 520 feet below ground, but was larger, approximately seven by seven feet.

The third tunnel was discovered on October 17,

1978. Unlike the previous ones, the third tunnel was discovered following a tip from a North Korean defector. This tunnel was about 5,200 feet long and about 240 feet below ground. Foreign visitors touring the South Korean DMZ may view the inside of this tunnel using a sloped access shaft.

A fourth tunnel was discovered on March 3, 1990, north of Haean town in the former Punchbowl battlefield. The tunnel's dimensions were seven by seven feet and it is 476 feet deep. The method of construction was almost identical in structure to the second and third tunnels.

"I'll email you this report," concluded Todd.

"So where do I fit into this?" asked Matt.

"Before I get into that," started Todd, "we want you to travel to North Korea as a tourist to get a feel for the place. We're not even considering any kind of operation north of the border; far too risky, but we have precious little firsthand knowledge of the Hermit Kingdom."

"Do I get a reward for that?" asked Matt.

Todd laughed and said, "Rewards are like hemorrhoids. Every asshole gets them at one time or another, but no rewards in this case. As for the hemorrhoids . . ."

"Enough said," smiled Matt, and continued, "I should take Federica with me. It adds credibility traveling as a tourist, and we should visit South Korea first. I've been there many times but it would get Federica acclimated somewhat to the culture and the food."

"OK," said Todd, "but don't go too crazy with your expenses. While you're away we'll be thinking about the next steps."

They called it a day and walked back to the Marriott. They met later in the lounge bar for drinks. Todd had made a reservation at the Maze Grill.

"I think you'll like it," Todd said, "it's a Gordon Ramsay restaurant, and it's within walking distance."

So they walked. They choose the same entrée, grilled Dover

sole with rosemary baby potatoes and sautéed spring greens, with a delightful chardonnay.

When they were nearing the end of their meal, Matt asked, "you ever been to Boodle's Gentlemen's club?"[12]

"No, Matt, but I've heard of it. I believe Ian Fleming and David Niven had memberships there."

"Amongst notable others," replied Matt, "it's the second oldest club in the world. It was founded in 1762, and Sir Winston Churchill was one of the few to be elected to honorary membership. I have a membership. Would you like a nightcap?"

"Sure," said Todd, "but how in the world did they let a guy like you in?"

"I have my father to thank for that," Matt answered.

"Out of interest," Todd asked, "what's the oldest club in the world?"

"That's White's," replied Matt, "it was founded in 1693 and it's a short walk from Boodle's on St. James's Street. Members include Prince Charles and Prince William; in fact Charles had his stag night there before his marriage to Lady Diana Spencer. It continues to be a men-only establishment; the only exception being made during a visit by Queen Elizabeth II in 1991."

"Is Boodle's men-only?" asked Todd.

"Yes and no," said Matt, "where we are going is men-only, but there is a women-only section with a distinct address and entrance."

"Bloody chauvinists you Brits," muttered Miller.

They hailed a cab to 28 St. James's Street and entered. They sat and just soaked in the atmosphere, imagining the discussions that must have taken place here over the years. As they sipped their cognacs Matt mentioned that Fleming had actually referred to the club in a few of his books, but had called it 'Blades.' After one more drink, they returned to the Marriott. Miller had found the experience rather intimidating.

Matt booked an alarm call for the morning. Federica was arriving on an early Air France flight, and he drove out to Heathrow

---

12   www.boodles.org.

to meet her. She looked devastating and he broke a few speed limits driving back to the hotel, where they devoured each other. Matt finally had the presence of mind to ask is she was hungry.

"I'm satiated, thanks, darling," she smiled, "but I'd love a strong coffee!"

Matt dutifully made two cups.

Federica had always wanted to visit Kew Gardens so they drove there and explored the best gardens either of them had ever seen, the world's largest collection of living plants, more than 30,000. They took a short break for lunch and made sure they visited the orchid collections, housed in two climate-controlled zones, before leaving. They were tired, drove back to the hotel, had a small dinner there, and slept in until calling room service for breakfast. Matt drove her to Heathrow and on the way, told her when they were both back in California, he wanted to plan a trip to visit South and North Korea.

"North Korea?" exclaimed Federica.

"A new experience for both of us," said Matt, smiling, and Federica reciprocated.

After parking, Matt wheeled her bags to the Air France check-in desk, kissed goodbye, and then drove back to the Marriott, stopping at a service station on the way to fill his tank.

Ellis had been informed of Talbot's movements but after calling the Marriott knew he had not yet checked out. He met Hassan's flight and drove him to Hertz where he picked up his Mini Cooper Works. Ellis handed him a package containing a handgun and spare ammunition, then left him to his own devices. Hassan thought he had made an excellent choice of car for the twists and turns of English country roads. Under normal circumstances he would have been correct, but he was unaware of the formidable capabilities of a Caterham 7.

Todd Miller called Talbot to let him know they had spotted Hassan as he arrived at Heathrow and he had rented a red Mini. Matt said he would plan on leaving his hotel late afternoon, planning to arrive close to his destination in Norfolk during darkness. He called his friends to let them know.

Matt asked for his car to be brought round to the hotel entrance as he checked out. Before leaving he had retrieved the handgun and night vision goggles from the safe in his suite, and now he had them secreted again in the front of the car. The London-based CIA agent, Steve Marcella, the chase guy, collected the BMW M3 he had reserved from the motor pool after picking up his weapon from the armory. He called Matt just to let him know he would be following Hassan discreetly in a metallic silver BMW.

It would be an interesting chase, Matt thought; three fast cars, driven by SAS, CIA and Al-Qaeda veterans across the English countryside.

Chapter 6
Chase through the Fens

The A10, UK, 2017

MATT WAS VERY FAMILIAR with the A10 route. He had traveled it hundreds of times and that gave him an advantage over Hassan. It was not the fastest way to reach his destination but he always enjoyed the mixture of dual carriageways and single-lane roads as they drove through quaint villages, small towns and rolling fields. It was rush-hour for the masochistic London workers driving home for a few hours' sleep before repeating the drudgery the following day. Matt was expecting this. It gave him the opportunity to watch out for Hassan's car. Sure enough he soon spotted a red Mini following, usually two or three cars behind. Once, when other cars had turned off, the Mini was right behind him temporarily and he managed to identify Hassan in his rear-view mirror. Hassan had no idea that his new identity was known to the CIA. Once in Cambridgeshire, the topography changed from undulating hills to flat agricultural and fenlands and Matt admired the acres of mustard fields as he drove by. There was still plenty of traffic, and it was highly unlikely that Hassan would try anything here. Matt stuck to the speed limits. When he stopped at a traffic light, he took the opportunity to take the night-vision goggles and SIG out from their hiding place and placed them by his side on the passenger seat. They drove round the villages of Melbourn and Foxton, through Harston and up the M11 and the A14 to get to the Milton interchange, bypassing Ely and Downham Market before reaching King's Lynn in Norfolk. Before darkness started to shroud them, Matt still had eyes on the red Mini and he caught an occasional glimpse in his mirror of the BMW in the distance. Now it was time to start having fun, as Talbot headed for the back roads, of which he had intimate knowledge. He let the Caterham have its head now that there was little traffic on the roads. The Mini did its best to follow, but every time it got close Talbot punched the accelerator and left it standing. The Mini used to be the king of rally driving but was no match for a well-driven 7, especially when Talbot kept playing with the switch that activated or deactivated the brake lights to throw off his quarry. The fens were full of tricky undulating and narrow roads and Matt recalled one spot that would serve his purposes admirably. He headed for Watlington Road that heads toward the station from Tilney St. Lawrence. He was driving toward a notorious accident black spot. He slowed a little, quickly switched off his brake lights again, and turned off his driving lights as he donned his night-vision goggles. He was to all intents invisible from a distance. He hit the gas again, accelerating toward a small humpback bridge. As soon as he over it, he slammed on his brakes and drifted round a sharp right turn. The Caterham oversteered but Talbot deftly recovered. He slowed to watch out for the Mini. As he expected, Hassan's car literally took off as it hit the apex of the bridge. Too late, he attempted to take the right turn but the car understeered and broadsided the drain at the side of the road. Talbot could see the Mini's headlight beams pointing toward the sky and wavering as the car rolled at least three times. Hassan must have felt as if he was having sex for the first time, thought Talbot; he had no idea what was happening and it was all over very quickly. Talbot drove a little farther and called Marcella, the BMW driver, and told him to slow down if he hadn't already. But Marcella had also seen the all-telling headlight beams in the sky and he drove carefully to inspect the scene, though he did not get out of the car to leave any indication of his visit. The Mini had suffered catastrophic damage, but he did not hang around. He drove a little farther, and then called Matt to make sure he was OK. Then he called Todd Miller, who told him to find a hotel for the night, and then drive back to London in the morning. "The strange thing was," said Marcella, "Talbot's car completely disappeared just before the accident. No lights. It was just as if he wasn't there." Miller called his counterpart in MI6 and suggested they look into an accident that had just taken place in Norfolk. The driver, dead or alive, was expected to be a Pakistani national, was suspected of being armed, and a member of Al-Qaeda. That got Cedric Jackson's attention. He alerted his agents and called the local police in Norfolk who had not yet heard about the accident, but immediately drove out to the scene with an ambulance that took Hassan to a hospital. They found the gun and a cellphone and bagged them as evidence for the MI6 guys.[13] Nothing appeared in the local press the next day, but the police met with the MI6 agents early in the morning and led them to the scene of the incident, where they took over. Guards were placed outside Hassan's hospital room. He was in critical condition with several broken bones and as-yet undetermined internal injuries.

Meanwhile, Talbot had congratulated himself on his well-executed plan, with no shots fired. He had switched on his lights, hidden the goggles and handgun under the seat again and continued toward Smeeth Road, where he made tracks to his friends' house in Walpole St. Peter. He arrived slightly early, no worse for wear.

---

13   MI6: The British equivalent of the USA's CIA.

Chapter 7
Relaxing with Friends

Norfolk, UK, 2017

RICHARD AND JENNIFER, friends since Matt's early twenties, greeted him before he even rang the doorbell and invited him in, but not before admiring the Caterham they had not seen in a few years.

"You made good time," said Richard, shaking hands with his old friend.

"Well, I had an incentive to get here quickly," Matt responded, as he hugged Jenny, who announced that she had made shepherd's pie, just the way he liked it.

"With minced lamb?" asked Matt, "when I can find it in the US they always seem to make it with minced beef!"

"Of course it's made with lamb," Jenny replied, "otherwise it would be cottage pie."

Matt just laughed. It was good to be back. They caught up on their recent exploits although there was much Matt could not talk about. The evening became night and they turned in.

Next morning, after a simple breakfast, they figured out what to do while Matt was on his brief visit. Matt's next hankering was for a lunch of fish and chips, which he had not enjoyed, English-style, for a few years. They went to a pub that served superb battered cod, the inevitable fat soggy chips, mushy peas, and the mandatory salt and malt vinegar, accompanied with room-temperature bitter beer. Heavenly! He was just finishing when his Apple Watch told him a call was incoming from Todd Miller. He excused himself and walked outside to take the call.

"What the fuck happened last night?" asked Todd.

"Nothing I couldn't handle!" responded Matt, "my SAS friend loaned me some night-vision goggles and combined with my knowledge of Norfolk backroads I put the guy in a ditch, or rather over the ditch, after some tricky driving. No shots fired."

"Now I understand what went down," said Todd, "you'll be pleased to hear he's still in hospital. No further reports."

Unlike Todd, Matt did trust his iPhone's security. Matt hung up but called Federica and left a voicemail to let her know he had reached Norfolk, asking her to call back when she could.

He rejoined his friends and they made plans to meet other friends for dinner the following evening at Congham Hall in Grimston, a place Matt had heard about often but had never had the good fortune to visit.[14] Congham Hall is steeped in history; a small but magnificent hotel, wonderful English gardens and menus to die for, always inclusive of homegrown vegetables. Elton John, apparently, had once booked the entire hotel and restaurant for a private function.

That evening they visited yet another local establishment, the King of Hearts, which always served a roast meal of some kind, this time lamb with all the trimmings, another delight that Matt enjoyed. He was being spoiled.

Matt received another call from Todd Miller the next morning, and had to go outside again to take the call. The CIA had received word from their guy in Syria whose source advised that funds had been transferred to a local representative working for North Korea. Sanctions put in place in 2015 had restricted resources for many of North Korea's foreign agents, but they always seemed to manage ways around such constraints. More information was not yet forthcoming, but the scuttlebutt was that they were trying to source sarin gas.

"Holy shit!" was Matt's response.

"Exactly," said Miller, "I'll keep you updated. Meanwhile, have a great time while you can."

Federica called Matt back a few minutes later. She was doing

---

14   www.conghamhallhotel.co.uk.

fine, just very busy. She was happy at being able to keep most of the clothes she was modeling.

"Sounds familiar," thought Matt, but he didn't say anything.

The next day, Matt, Richard and Jenny met their mutual friends, four other couples, and they converged on Congham Hall. They enjoyed a magnificent meal, some choosing roast pork with crackling, some roast lamb, some roast beef and Yorkshire pudding, and others Dover sole, all with the highly anticipated garden vegetables. He endured several questions about Federica, who his friends had never met, promising to fix that as soon as possible.

But the next day, Matt was feeling a bit anxious with all that was going on and decided to cut his short vacation even shorter. He called British Airways and booked his return flight to LAX, made his excuses to his dear friends, and drove to Heathrow to meet Mark Smyth, returning the ever-faithful Caterham, including the hidden equipment. He bade him farewell for the moment, promising to be in touch again soon, and walked to the check-in desk. He made his way to the first class lounge after passing through security and left a brief voicemail for Miller, then relaxed and helped himself to snacks and a scotch before boarding.

Matt checked his email as soon as they were airborne and there was one from Todd Miller, who wanted to visit him in California. Federica was not due back for about another three days so that would work out just fine. He reflected on his 'vacation.' It had been a busy few days and he'd managed to catch up with several really good friends who had touched his life in different ways. And he had to admit he had experienced a rush of adrenaline during the brush with Hassan. But he didn't raise his hopes about the asshole's demise. Until or unless he heard otherwise, he would assume that Hassan's removal from this earth was about as permanent as a fart in a wind tunnel. He ordered another drink and instead of having a full formal meal, opted for the lighter bistro selection. Then he slept until being woken for afternoon tea before landing at LAX. There was a selection of delicious sandwiches, and scones with clotted cream and strawberry preserves, but he refused the Twining teas after consuming so much over the last few days and ordered a cappuccino.

Chapter 8
Back in La Jolla

California, 2017

MATT'S LEARJET HAD BEEN waiting for him at LAX and before he knew it he was back at home in La Jolla Farms. His housekeeper had left him a note. His mail was stacked on his kitchen counter as usual and Winston, his dog, had been fed and walked. He asked Winston to fetch him a drink but apparently he had still not learned that trick so Matt fetched one for himself. He watched TV for a little while and went to bed.

Todd Miller called early the next morning from a CIA Learjet, on his way to California. Matt said he would be at Montgomery Field when he landed and invited him to stay at his house. He took Federica's Lotus.

"You addicted to Lotus now?" asked Todd sarcastically.

Matt just ignored him and drive home. His housekeeper had stocked him up with basic supplies including a French baguette so they had a simple lunch of bread, ham, cheese, and pickles, then got down to business.

"First order of business," opened Todd, "your nemesis Hassan. I called Cedric Jackson, my MI6 friend, on the way here. Hassan was badly hurt but will recover eventually. He suffered several broken ribs, a busted collar bone, and a fractured hip. He also has damage to his liver. MI6 went through his cell phone and found plenty to incriminate him. As soon as he's recovered enough, he'll be deported to Pakistan and he'll be placed on the UK and US no-fly lists."

"That won't stop him," said Matt, "can't we take him out?"

"Not while he's in the UK," said Todd, "that would not be politically correct while he's in MI6 custody."

"Fuck politics," thought Matt, but he kept quiet, instead asking, "have the Pakistani authorities been advised he's Al-Qaeda?"

"Yes," replied Todd, "but that doesn't guarantee they'll do anything as history tells us."

"Wonderful," said Matt, "just wonderful. When will those guys wake up to what's going on, on their doorsteps? Bin Laden should have been a wake-up call and that was a long time ago."

"Shit happens," said Todd, "as hard as we try we can't change the world."

"I'll get that prick if it's the last thing I do," muttered Matt quietly, but loud enough for Todd to hear.

"I know you will," said Todd, "but not while he's in the hands of our allies."

"Next item,'" said Todd, "gas."

"Bathroom's over there," said Matt.

"Can you be serious for a minute?" asked Todd, "I'm talking about sarin gas. We now know for sure that North Korea has a lethal quantity, but we don't have any idea what they're planning to do with it. We have a team working night and day to try to figure out what they might be up to. Do you have any idea how disgusting this stuff is?"

"As a matter of fact I do, Todd. I did some research of my own, in between enjoying myself on vacation before it was rudely interrupted."

"Point taken," said Todd. "But before you tell me what you've learned, a few words about Syria. Damascus is the capital of the country, as you know, known officially as the Syrian Arab Republic. The population is largely Sunni Arabs. In 2007, Israeli jet fighters carried out Operation Orchard against a suspected nuclear reactor under construction by North Korean technicians, displaying to the world the worrying and growing relationship between two of the biggest abusers of human rights. In 2013 Syria was suspected of using heinous chemical weapons against its own people, likely sarin gas. Since then, of course, the level of violence ratcheted up with ISIS coming into the picture, Russia and the US almost coming to blows over their support of warring factions, and the horrendous migrant issues that the world is still dealing with. The country is in complete shambles, giving North Korea, for instance, almost anything they want from the fallout."

"Scary as hell, the worst humanitarian crisis since WW II," was about all Talbot could say, as he opened his iPad to reference his notes. "Here's what I found out about sarin," he said.

> It's a colorless, odorless liquid, used as a chemical weapon owing to its extreme potency as a nerve agent and was classified as a weapon of mass destruction in UN Resolution 687. Production and stockpiling of sarin was outlawed as of April 1997 by the Chemical Weapons Convention of 1993.
>
> Sarin can be lethal even at very low concentrations, with death following within one to ten minutes after direct inhalation due to suffocation from lung muscle paralysis, unless some antidotes, typically atropine or biperiden and pralidoxime, are quickly administered to a victim. Anyone who absorbs a nonlethal dose, but does not receive immediate, radical treatment, may suffer permanent neurological damage.
>
> Sarin degrades after a period of several weeks to several months. In binary chemical weapons, two precursors are stored separately in the same container and mixed to form the agent immediately before deployment. This approach has the dual benefit of solving the stability issue and increasing the safety of sarin munitions.
>
> The effects of exposure to sarin are rapid and devastating. Initial symptoms are a runny nose, tightness in the chest and constriction of the pupils. Soon after, the victim has difficulty breathing and experiences nausea and drooling. As the victim continues to lose control of bodily functions, vomiting, defecation and

urination follow, then twitching and jerking. Ultimately, the victim becomes comatose and suffocates in a series of convulsive spasms.

Sarin was discovered in Wuppertal-Elberfeld in Germany by scientists at IG Farben who were attempting to create stronger pesticides. In mid-1939, the formula for the agent was passed to the chemical warfare section of the German Army Weapons Office, which ordered that it be brought into mass production for wartime use. Pilot plants were built, and a high-production facility was under construction (but was not finished) by the end of WWII. Thankfully, Germany never did use nerve agents against Allied targets.

In the early 1950s NATO adopted sarin as a standard chemical weapon, and both the USSR and the US produced the chemical for military purposes. Production of sarin in the US ceased in 1956, but it was not until 1993 that the UN banned the production and stockpiling of many chemical weapons, including sarin, and called for the complete destruction of stockpiles by 2007. But it never quite went away. The most recent publicized event was in 2013, when sarin was used in an attack in the Ghouta region of the Rif Dimashq Governorate of Syria during the Syrian civil war.

"Nothing to add to that," said Miller. "Jesus, what are those bastards up to?"

"Next subject," said Todd.

"Coffee," said Matt, and walked to his Gaggia, his pride and joy.

"What the hell does that thing do?" asked Todd sarcastically.

"Last time I used it, it made real coffee, unlike that crap you usually drink. Federica bought it for me."

Todd said nothing, but enjoyed the best cappuccino he had ever had a few minutes later. He never stopped learning from Talbot, but would be the last to admit it.

"OK, next real subject," said Miller, "the tunnel. We don't want to stop the Koreans digging yet, until we figure out their objective. But we need to get eyes on their activities. They're making slow but steady progress. After many brainstorming sessions, we figured the best way is to do some drilling of our own, under the pretext of searching for coal. We sought advice from some of the best mining experts in the country and discovered how to drill narrow holes quietly and deeply."

"So what's the point of that?" asked Matt.

"We are sinking fiber-optic cables with both optical and audio sensors so we can see and hear what they're up to," replied Todd. "We sank one hole close to the start of the tunnel on our side, but just out of sight from the DMZ, then are spacing others following the course of the tunnel as they lengthen it. We're recording their activities. The mining guys even have a vacuum gadget that they can sink beside the drill head to suck up rock particles and dust to prevent them from falling into the tunnel."

"Aren't you worried about drones," Matt asked.

"In short, no," replied Todd. "North Korea has built some, and they tried spying on us south of the border, but they were easy to spot and we simply shot them down. In fact, the army installed a Patriot battery for the sole purpose of detecting and destroying any future drones.[15] None have been seen for about six months now."

"Why do you need me?" asked Matt, "sounds as though you've got all the expertise you need, and I know squat about mining."

"We just want you to take a look after your 'vacation' in North Korea," said Todd, "we want you to understand the lay of the land ready for when we need to take overt action. We may or may not need you for that action, but will certainly appreciate your advice, in any event."

"Fair enough," said Matt, "guess I'll be eating lots of kimchi over the next few weeks."

"Talking of which," asked Todd, "have you done any planning yet for the trip to Korea?"

"Of course not, Todd. I just came back from the UK, and then

---

15 The MIM-104 Patriot is a surface-to-air missile system.

you arrived. I have often been asked to do the impossible, but miracles take a little longer. Over the next few days, before Federica arrives, I intend to plan the trip, get in some target practice, and try to shed some weight I put on eating fattening Brit food!"

"OK, OK," sighed Todd.

"Last subject," said Todd. "We've been increasingly frustrated, embarrassed and appalled by the North's ever-vigilant cyber-hacking exploits. The NSA guys are tearing their hair out, though they've had a few recent successes at foiling some attempts. My team, together with the NSA, has put together a report that I'll share with you. I think you'll find it both interesting and scary. We want to mount a covert operation to put their hacking operation out of business for a very long time, and we need you and your team for that."

"You want me to mount an operation in North Korea?" exclaimed Matt.

"No, in China," replied Todd.

"Time for dinner," said Matt, as that sank in. "First, a drink. What's your poison?"

"Jack Daniels, if you have it, on the rocks," said Todd.

"Coming up," said Matt as he poured himself a Johnnie Walker Blue, neat. "I have porterhouse steaks, corn on the cob and baking potatoes in the fridge if that sounds OK," suggested Matt, "we can use the barbecue by the pool."

"Sounds great," said Todd, "I'll give you a hand."

They relaxed by the pool for the evening and enjoyed the food and drinks. Matt talked about his car chase through the fens in Norfolk and Todd talked excitedly about the baby boy soon to come into his life. The problems of the world were forgotten for a few hours.

The next morning over breakfast Todd told Matt he had emailed the report about the hackers for him to digest over the next few days. Matt invited Todd to join him for target practice, and to his surprise he accepted after calling his pilot to delay the flight. Matt unlocked his gun cabinet; they took a couple of M4A1 carbines, jumped in Matt's old F150 and headed to the desert.

Matt set up targets. Todd went first. When they walked over to the targets they were both pleasantly surprised at Todd's accuracy since he was out of practice, but Matt won the day. They stayed for about one hour, then Todd received a text from his pilot telling him that he was wanted urgently back in Langley. Matt drove him to the airfield and he changed on the plane.

Matt drove home and opened up the hacker report.

Chapter 9
The Hacker Report

California, 2017

Back in early 2015, the trail that led American officials to blame North Korea for the destructive cyberattack on Sony Pictures Entertainment in November went back to 2010, when the NSA had scrambled to break into the computer systems of a country considered one of the most impenetrable targets on earth.

Spurred by growing concerns about North Korea's maturing capabilities, the American spy agency drilled into the Chinese networks that connect North Korea to the outside world, tracing connections through Malaysia favored by North Korean hackers, and penetrated directly into the North with the help of South Korea and other American allies.

A classified security agency program expanded into an ambitious effort, officials said, to place malware that could track the internal workings of many of the computers and networks used by the North's hackers, a force that South Korea's military claimed to number roughly 6,000 people. Most are commanded by the country's main intelligence service, called the Reconnaissance General Bureau (RGB) and Bureau 121, its secretive hacking unit, with a large outpost in China. The RGB itself falls under the Ministry of People's Armed Forces that in turn is part of the National

Defense Commission (NDC). RGB operated for years in traditional espionage and clandestine operations before morphing into cyber operations. Several other cyber units operate under North Korea's other arm of government, the Worker's Party of Korea (WPK). Unit 35 is responsible for training cyber agents who handle domestic cyber investigations and operations. Unit 204 takes part in online espionage and psychological warfare and Office 225 trains agents for missions in South Korea, sometimes including cyberattacks. North Korea's school system emphasizes mathematics from a very young age, and the most gifted students are given access to computers. The best programmers go to a handful of schools having specialist computer departments, typically Kim Il Sung University, the country's most prestigious seat of learning, or Kim Chaek University of Technology, or Mirim College. Students specialize in disciplines such as cyber warfare. After graduation they are often sent overseas for further studies, and participate in hackers' forums. North Korea has only one connection to the Internet and uses computers around the globe to launch attacks. Compromised PCs often show no sign of infection by North Korean malware, thought to be launched from outposts in China, Russia and India. Other than the famous attack on Sony, there have been many others, mostly targeted at financial institutions. There are only about 1000 Internet users in the country itself, limited to elite students, scientists and foreigners.

The evidence gathered by the "early warning radar" of software painstakingly hidden to monitor North Korea's activities proved critical in persuading President Obama to accuse the government of Kim Jong-un of ordering the Sony attack, according to the officials and experts, who spoke on the condition of anonymity about the classified NSA operation.

The president's decision to accuse North Korea of ordering the largest destructive attack against an American target - and to promise retaliation, which soon began in the form of new economic sanctions - was highly unusual: the United States had previously never explicitly charged another government with mounting a cyberattack on American targets.

Mr. Obama was cautious in drawing stark conclusions from intelligence, aides said, but in this case, 'he had no doubt,' according to senior officials.

For about a decade, the US had implanted 'beacons,' which could map a computer network, along with surveillance software and occasionally even destructive malware in the computer systems of foreign adversaries. The government spends billions of dollars on the technology, which was crucial to the American and Israeli attacks on Iran's nuclear program, and documents previously disclosed by Edward J. Snowden, the former security agency contractor, demonstrated how widely they have been deployed against China.

But fearing the exposure of its methods to a country that remains a black hole for intelligence gathering, American officials have declined to talk publicly about the role the technology played in Washington's assessment that the North Korean government had ordered the attack on Sony.

The NSA's success in getting into North Korea's systems should have allowed the agency to see the initial 'spear phishing' attacks on Sony - the use of emails that placed malicious code into a computer system if an unknowing user clicks on a link - when the attacks first began.

But those attacks did not look unusual. Only in retrospect did investigators determine that the North had stolen the 'credentials' of a Sony systems administrator, which allowed the hackers to roam freely inside

Sony's systems. Investigators concluded that the hackers spent more than two months mapping Sony's computer systems, identifying critical files and planning how to destroy computers and servers.

'They were incredibly careful and patient,' said a person briefed on the investigation. But he added that even with their view into the North's activities, American Intelligence agencies couldn't really understand the severity of the destruction that was coming when the attacks actually started.

Jang Sae-yul, a former North Korean army programmer who defected in 2007, speaking in an interview in Seoul, said: 'They have built up formidable hacking skills. They have spent almost 30 years getting ready, learning how to do this and this alone, how to target specific countries.'

The FBI director stated that the IP addresses being used to post and send the emails were coming from IPs that were exclusively used by the North Koreans, and some of those addresses appear to have been in China. He continued to say that there was other conclusive evidence that could not be disclosed, and there was no question in their minds.

Defectors say that the Internet was first viewed by North Korea's leadership as a threat, something that could taint its citizens with outside ideas. But Kim Heung-kwang, a defector who said in an interview that he helped train many of the North's first cyber spies, recalled that in the early 1990s a group of North Korean computer experts came back from China with a 'very strange new idea': use the Internet to steal secrets and attack the government's enemies. 'The Chinese are already doing it,' he quoted.

Defectors report that the North Korean military was interested. So was the ruling WPK, which in 1994 sent fifteen North Koreans to a military academy in Beijing to learn about hacking. When they returned, they formed the core of the External Information Intelligence Office, which hacked into websites, penetrated firewalls and stole information overseas. Because the North had so few connections to the outside world, the hackers did much of their work in China.

According to Mr. Kim, the military began training computer 'warriors' in earnest in 1996 and two years later opened Bureau 121, now the primary cyberattack unit. Members were dispatched for two years of training in China and Russia. Mr. Hang said they were envied, in part because of their freedom to travel. 'They used to come back with exotic foreign clothes and expensive electronics like rice cookers and cameras,' he said. The border with China had become increasingly porous. His friends told him that Bureau 121 was divided into different groups, each targeting a specific country or region, especially the United States, South Korea and the North's sole ally, China.

'They spent those two years not attacking, but just learning about their target country's Internet,' said Mr. Jang, a first lieutenant in a different army unit that wrote software for war game simulations.

Mr. Jang said that as time went on, the North began diverting high-school students with the best math skills into a handful of top universities, including Miram University, a military school specializing in computer-based warfare, which he attended as a young army officer.

Others were deployed to an 'attack base' in the northeastern Chinese city of Shenyang, where there are many North Korean-run hotels and restaurants. Unlike the North's nuclear and ballistic missile programs, the cyber forces could be used to harass South Korea and the United States without risking devastating reprisals.

'Cyber warfare is simply the modern chapter in North Korea's long history of asymmetrical warfare,' said a security research report issued by Hewlett Packard.

When the Americans first gained access to the North Korean networks and computers in 2010, their surveillance focused on the North's nuclear program and its leadership, and efforts to detect attacks aimed at United States military forces in South Korea, said one former American official. Then a highly destructive attack in 2013 on South Korean banks and media companies suggested that North Korea was becoming a greater threat, and the focus shifted.

'The big target was the hackers,' the official said.

That attack knocked out almost 50,000 computers and servers in South Korea for several days at five banks and television broadcasters.

The hackers were patient, spending nine months probing the South Korean systems. But they also made the mistake seen in the Sony hack, at one point revealing what South Korean analysts believe to have been their true IP addresses. Lim Jong-in, dean of the Graduate School of Information Security at Korea University, said those addresses were traced back to Shenyang, and fell within a spectrum of IP addresses linked to North Korean companies.

The attack was studied by American intelligence agencies. But after the North issued its warnings about Sony's crude comedy 'The Interview,' about a CIA plot to assassinate the North's leader, being an 'act of war,' American officials appear to have made no reference to the risk in their discussions with Sony executives. Even when the spear-phishing attacks began - against Sony and other targets - 'it didn't set off alarm bells,' according to one person involved in the investigation.

The result was that American officials began to focus

on North Korea only after the destructive attacks began, when pictures of skulls and gruesome images of Sony executives appeared on the screens of company employees. That propaganda move by the hackers may have worked to Sony's benefit: some employees unplugged their computers immediately, saving some data from destruction.

It did not take long for American officials to conclude that the source of the attack was North Korea, officials say. 'Figuring out how to respond was a lot harder,' one White House official said. But reprisals there were, with a wave of fresh sanctions.

'We take North Korea's attack that aimed to create destructive financial effects on a US Company and to threaten artists and other individuals with goal of restricting their right to free expression very seriously,' the White House Press Secretary said in a statement. 'As the president has said, our response to North Korea's attack against Sony Pictures Entertainment will be proportional, and will take place at a time and in a manner of our choosing. Today's actions are the first aspect of our response.'

An executive order signed by President Obama authorized sanctions against agencies and officials associated with the North Korean government and Workers Party of Korea. Obama, in the order, cited North Korea's 'provocative, destabilizing, and repressive actions and policies, including its destructive, coercive cyber-related actions during November and December of 2014.'

The Treasury Department, in turn, designated three government-tied entities and ten North Korean officials under those sanctions. The sanctions denied them access to the US financial system and barred them from entering the US.

The department did not name North Korean leader

Kim Jong-un but did designate representatives of the government stationed in Russia, Iran and Syria, among others. It also named North Korea's primary intelligence organization, its primary arms dealer and an organization that deals with technology procurement called the Korea Tangun Trading Corporation.

North Korea was already subject to other U.S. sanctions related to its nuclear program, and coupled with the additional actions taken, served to further isolate key North Korean entities and disrupt the activities of close to a dozen critical operatives.

"Oh my god," muttered Matt. "Now what the fuck have I got myself into?"

Chapter 10
Planning the Visit to the Hermit Kingdom

La Jolla, California, 2017

MATT HAD BEEN TO South Korea countless times, mostly Seoul, but had no real feel for the Hermit Kingdom other than what he had seen and read online, and the somewhat limited coverage afforded by other media.

He called his friend Alan, who lived close by, and invited him over. Alan had taken a hiking tour in North Korea in 2008, and Matt needed to know more about his experiences.

Alan had traveled to Seoul first where he completed all the paperwork necessary for his adventure, the scariest of which was a document that stated in part, "The visit to the Joint Security Area (JSA) at Panmunjom will entail entry into a hostile area and the possibility of injury or death as a direct action of enemy action." He traveled to the Korean Demilitarized Zone (DMZ) where he boarded a bus with his fellow travelers and the ever-present guards and they drove to the JSA checkpoint. The JSA is the only portion of the DMZ where North and South Korean forces stand face-to-face. The checkpoint is used by the two Koreas for diplomatic engagements and, until March 1991, was also the site of military negotiations between North Korea and the United Nations Command (UNC). The JSA is located in what was the village of Panmunjom, no longer inhabited since it was destroyed during the war; now all that remains of the village is the building constructed for the signing of the armistice agreement in 1953, the North Korea Peace Museum. The new visitors were surrounded by floodlights in what looked like a concentration camp. Guards were everywhere. Anyone caught taking photographs were sent back to the border. Their possessions were thoroughly searched. Cameras were taken away but later returned. Any literature or maps were confiscated.

When they re-boarded the bus they saw wide roads but few private vehicles. Lots of bicycles with baskets but strangely they were being pushed, not ridden. There were pretty girls acting as tourist guides, apparently selected and trained from a very young age. Their cameras were returned so they could take pictures of the girls and other attractions pointed out to them. They were not allowed to ask questions other than those that related to their itinerary or weather conditions. There were very strictly policed designated smoking areas. Anyone breaking the rules was whisked off somewhere. They stayed at a rudimentary tourist hotel for the first night, after which they slept in tents when the hike proper started up the Gold River Mountain.

They continued to Pyongyang where they were escorted to a huge symphony hall and witnessed a truly spectacular acrobatic act given by young men and women who had also been specially selected and trained from a very young age. The group was told that the acrobats performed worldwide and were some of the best-paid people in the country. The acrobats performed with no harnesses or safety nets and their expertise exceeded that of the best Cirque de Soleil acts Alan had ever seen in Las Vegas, accompanied by an amazing live orchestra.

After the performance the group was encouraged to take photographs of shrines to Kim Jong-il.

Each member of the group had to wear an identification tag with their name, photograph and the dates of their permitted stay, and a guard was watching over each of them for the entire visit. The food was similar to that eaten in the South so no surprises there and they drank soju and locally produced beer. The language spoken was not quite the same, however, having Chinese roots rather the phonetic Hangul language used in the South. This all sounded rather intimidating, but at no time did anyone feel threatened so long as they abided by the rules.

These bus tours only ran between 2003 and 2008, and were then canceled. Private vehicles are never allowed to cross the DMZ. Matt thanked Alan for his help and he returned home.

Talbot would need to fly to North Korea from Beijing for his visit, and he found a tour company that specialized in such trips. While some itineraries focus on less-visited areas in the country's north, such as North Hamgyong Province (the province where North Korea is reported to conduct its nuclear tests) and the Rason Special Economic Zone (an area near the Chinese and Russian borders established in the early 1990s to promote economic growth through foreign investment), the majority are focused on the country's capital of Pyongyang and the DMZ with South Korea. He chose the latter.

Talbot quickly discovered, to his surprise, that even as a US Citizen, signing up for a tour was as easy as filling out a few forms online and wiring money to reserve their places on a tour. He used Beijing-based, British-led, Koryo Tours for all the arrangements including the preparation of paperwork for their visas. He learned that Koryo were partners of the Korean International Tourist Company (KITC), a North Korean government-run organization that employs the Korean guides who would accompany them while in-country. Matt busied himself finalizing everything with Koryo Tours and booking flights and hotels en-route. He aimed to have everything in process by the time Federica returned, and when they had both recovered from jet-lag they would be ready to leave.

Chapter 11
Back to the Kimchi

The Koreas, 2017

FEDERICA HAD EMAILED her itinerary and Matt dutifully met her flight at the airport. He took the Bentley this time because he knew she would be overloaded with luggage.

They took it easy for a few days until the visas were finalized, then packed for the trip. Matt called Peter, his pilot, and they flew to LAX in his Learjet. The nonstop flight to Seoul was uneventful and in first class Korean Air was superb as always. A limousine was waiting after they cleared immigration and customs and they were taken to the W Seoul Hotel on Walkerhill. Matt had stayed at the JW Marriott on previous visits but the W had been recommended and they were not disappointed. After they had relaxed Matt took Federica out to sample bulgogi, one his favorite Korean dishes. Bulgogi is one of Korea's most popular beef dishes, made from thinly sliced sirloin or ribeye. It is usually marinated in a mixture of soy sauce, sesame oil, black pepper, garlic, onions, ginger and sugar for two to four hours to enhance the flavor and its tenderization. Bulgogi is traditionally grilled over a brazier, with cloves of garlic, sliced onions, and chopped green peppers. It is usually served with lettuce or other leafy vegetables, used to wrap the slices of cooked meat. They also enjoyed kimchi, cabbage fermented with radish, garlic, chili peppers, green onions, ginger, salt and sugar, with other side dishes of diced radish kimchi, seasoned bean sprouts, braised tofu, and of course steamed rice. They washed everything down with OB (Oriental Brewery) beer, brewed from rice rather than the malted barley familiar to Western beer drinkers. And such a meal would be incomplete without soju, made from rice, wheat, or barley and typically 20% alcohol. They learned that soju was commonly called nongtaegi in North Korea and was often home-brewed and could reach an alcohol content of 25-30%! Matt warned Federica to take it easy with the potent stuff, after drunken experiences during previous visits to Seoul. Federica enjoyed most of her meal, but took a dislike to kimchi, an acquired taste. As soon as they returned to the hotel they needed a shower and a complete change of clothes after the fumes from the cooking experience, particularly the surfeit of garlic.

Shopping was the priority the next day and then Matt and Federica were hosted for lunch at the officers club in the US Army base in Itaewon by Matt's old friend Colonel Joe Howard. They prepared to fly to Beijing early in the morning. Matt had booked a suite in the opulent Raffles Beijing Hotel and one of their first tasks was to shop for bottled water, snacks and gifts (cigarettes had been recommended) for the guides when they reached North Korea. And just in case they took toilet paper, since apparently it was frequently unavailable outside Pyongyang. Matt reminded Federica that their belongings could be searched on entering North Korea, including files on their iPhones and iPads. Anything deemed offensive, however innocuous, would be deleted. The Hermit Kingdom is extremely conservative and they took appropriate clothing. No plunging necklines or short skirts for Federica!

Talbot had made bookings on North Korean flag carrier Air Koryo, which uses primarily Russian-made Tupolev TU-204s and, to a lesser extent, Ilyushin aircraft. They left on an early afternoon flight from Beijing Capital Airport's Terminal 2 for the roughly two-hour flight to Pyongyang Sunan International Airport. They were served an inflight meal, kind of, consisting of a cold hamburger of questionable origin and were given copies of the English-language Pyongyang Times to read. When leaving the aircraft they had been warned not to photograph anything relating to the military otherwise the consequences could be severe.

Having cleared customs without any issues they were directed to the single conveyor belt to collect their luggage before being introduced to their guide, who spoke excellent English.

Before they left the airport, they purchased SIM cards for their cell phones; they had been pretty amazed during their briefing that visiting foreigners could do this, but had warned close friends and colleagues to use burner phones if they needed to call. Apparently a mere 10% of the population owned cell phones but they could only be used for domestic calls, with no smartphone functionality or Internet access. They had been booked into the Yanggakdo International Hotel, a 47-story structure (the second-tallest building in North Korea) built by France's Campenon Bernard Construction Company, that boasts 1,001 rooms. Amazingly, the hotel had a bowling alley, spa, karaoke facilities, post center, in-house tailor and dry cleaner, massage parlor, pool hall, bar, revolving restaurant on the top floor (which offers incredible views of Pyongyang), several small stores selling items such as pins and books written by Kim Il Sung and Kim Jong-il, and even an underground casino. In the ornate lobby, there was a sea turtle in an aquarium. The windowed, carpeted rooms were also rather pleasant, with twin queen beds and warm blankets and a full bathroom (with working hot water and electricity) being standard. There was a TV that could receive international channels such as the BBC, as well as locally produced Korean Central Television (KCTV), and a telephone, though it was unknown whether calls were monitored; they didn't use it. But for all its opulent massiveness, they did not sneak out at night: the hotel lobby was staffed by a uniformed doorman, and even if they were to elude his watchful gaze, the Yanggakdo is on an island only accessible by a single bridge; get caught, and you could find yourself in serious trouble. North Korean citizens were not permitted to visit the casino. A moot point, thought Matt, since they could not afford to set foot in such a hotel, least of all stay there or gamble. The average per-capita annual income is $1-2K, compared to more than $20K in South Korea.

While in North Korea, they were at the mercy of their guides;

their word was law. While some rules (such as only taking pictures of statues from the front side, and including the entire statue in the photograph) may have seemed odd, they understood that the guides themselves could have gotten in trouble had they broken the rules.

Sumptuous meals of everything from kimchi to crabs and, had they felt so inclined, dog (though it's never a surprise and quite expensive to order), and lots and lots of rice, was the fare that they ate. There were also gallons of tea and alcoholic beverages, including North Korean-produced beer and soju. Venues for meals included one of the restaurants at the Yanggakdo, a microbrewery in Pyongyang and a pizza parlor.

Their itinerary was a busy one, each day a whirlwind of monuments, museums, and more stories about the Kim family than they ever thought imaginable. They saw the USS Pueblo (the US Navy spy ship captured in 1968 that holds the distinction of being the only US naval vessel currently held by an enemy), the bustling Pyongyang Metro (a two-line, 17-station subway system chock-full of socialist realist artwork) and performances by local schoolchildren; there was never a dull moment.

Before they left the country, they took a brief trip to the DMZ, from the north side this time. Although dubbed the "scariest border in the world" by National Geographic, there was little to fear: as the guides told them beforehand, the North Korean soldiers there (allegedly the tallest people in the North Korean military, to psychologically intimidate South Korean and US military) protected them. The DMZ was the only place they were allowed to take pictures of (and even with) soldiers. DMZ is a contradiction in terms mused Talbot. Heavily Militarized Zone would be far more appropriate.

After eight long days, the trip came to an end. They packed their bags, said farewell to their guides, and returned to the airport where they gave up their North Korean visas before boarding their flight back to Beijing. Their visas had been issued on separate documents, leaving no trace of their visit in their passports. Once again they stared in wonder at the airport, illustrating the dilemma facing the regime. It had obviously been constructed purely to facilitate the arrival of millions of visitors clutching wads of dollars and euros.

They returned to the Raffles Hotel in Beijing and enjoyed drinks while discussing their experiences for the first time. While the tour was fascinating, they not really learned anything about day-to-day life in the secretive kingdom. The guides had gone to extreme lengths to show the tour members only what they wanted them to see, with no hints of ongoing nuclear tests, human rights violations, arbitrary detentions of tourists, and bellicose rhetoric from the government threatening to transform places such as Seoul into a sea of fire. They had, however, seen occasional hints of capitalism creeping in. Though most of Pyongyang was in darkness quite early in the evening, given the shortage of electricity, an occasional solar panel could be spotted on the balconies of some apartments. And some enterprising residents were apparently starting to grow their own food and were trading. Most surprising though was the total lack of evidence of the worst drought in history facing the country, as reported outside of the country. More than thirty percent of rice paddies were parching up but they saw nothing. Following frequent and significant food shortages, about one-third of children in the country were malnourished and many suffered from stunted growth. In the past, many countries including, surprisingly, South Korea, had donated aid, but this had diminished greatly as Pyongyang developed nuclear weapons. Spending by UN agencies has fallen from $300M a year to the current $50M, after imposing severe sanctions given ongoing nuclear and missile tests dating back to 2006.

Meanwhile, Kim Jong-un lived a life of luxury, enjoying the finer things of life and preaching the prowess of the country to anyone who would listen. Although his whereabouts are for the most part concealed, it became known that his primary home (one of many), is Ryongsong Residence in northern Pyongyang, in a complex of almost five square miles. It was completed in 1983 under the rule of Kim Il-sung and was later used by Kim

Jong-il before Kim Jong-un succeeded his father. The complex has an underground wartime headquarters, protected with walls reinforced with iron rods and concrete covered with lead in case of nuclear attack. There are numerous military units to protect the headquarters stationed around the complex in possession of mass-scale conventional weapons. The area is surrounded by an electric fence, minefields and many security checkpoints. The headquarters is connected with other residences by tunnels, and a private underground train station is also inside the residence compound. Besides large houses and well-tended gardens there are man-made lakes and various recreational facilities, including banquet halls on the lakefront, a huge swimming pool, running track and athletic field, spa and sauna, horse stables and riding area, shooting range and an automobile racetrack. Witnesses have described luxurious interiors with ornate furnishings, deep plush carpets and fancy chandeliers.

Matt and Federica replaced the SIM cards in their phones, quickly checked urgent voicemails and emails, and went for a Chinese meal in the hotel. Kimchi was all well and good, but only in moderation.

Halfway through the meal, Matt said, "I feel between a wok and a hard place."

"If you mean what I think you mean," said Federica, smiling sexily, "we'd better finish quickly and go back to the room."

They finally made love for the first time in several days before falling into a long dreamless sleep.

During the flight home the next day, Matt sent an email to Todd, relating his brief impressions of the regime, but most details could wait until he got back.

Chapter 12
Visiting Langley

Virginia, 2017

ONE OF MATT'S FIRST TASKS on reaching home was to donate Jessica's clothes that had occupied much of his closet space since her untimely death.[16] He regained lots of storage space and earned lots of brownie points since Federica seemed to be leaving more and more clothes in his house. By this time, Federica and Winston, Matt's faithful Bouvier des Flandres, had become the best of friends, and he followed her everywhere she went.

Inevitably, Todd Miller called the next day. When he received the alert on his Apple Watch, Talbot was tempted to ignore it temporarily but caved in as usual. He sorely needed another impossible mission.

"Hi, Todd," he said, when he got through, "what a surprise!"

"Did I detect a note of sarcasm?" Todd asked.

"What can I do you for?" asked Matt.

"Can you fly to Langley as soon as possible?" asked Todd, "after a full debriefing on your paid 'vacation,' I need to talk about the 'mining' operation in South Korea and brief you on China."

"Can you give me a couple of days to wind down from the last trip?" he asked, "and Federica is getting ready to fly to Italy to visit friends and family. I was hoping to go with her, but you sound concerned."

"I am," said Todd, "let me know when you've figured things out. I can book a local hotel for you when you tell me your itinerary."

---

16   See *A Case for Drones*, a Matt Talbot adventure.

Matt cut the call, and broke the news that something had come up and he had to take a business trip, and sadly could not accompany her to Italy. She was growing used to this, and just shrugged her shoulders and pouted.

They dined out that evening and had an early night. Federica booked her flight to Milan on Alitalia the next day and Matt called his pilots to prepare to fly to Langley.

Federica arranged for a limo since Matt needed to leave first. They embraced and he drove to Montgomery field again. He checked his email while in flight but found nothing of consequence, and sent his ETA to Todd. He slept as best he could and drank coffee before landing at Langley Air Force base and undergoing the usual security checks, then Todd was there to escort him to their meeting room where lunch was waiting. This time Todd, or rather the cook, had excelled himself, and there were Cornish pasties and other treats waiting. This was ominous, Matt thought, there must be bad news coming.

Matt started by giving a full account of his observations while in North Korea.

"The biggest surprise to me," Matt recalled, "was the apparent adoration showered upon Kim Jong-un by the millions of people who barely eke out a living and many of whom are starving. I was reminded of what I know about the USSR during the Cold War when the general populace was also shielded from living conditions outside their world. But what I witnessed in Korea was far worse."

"It's a culture we can only try to comprehend," remarked Todd, "children are taught from a very young age that the Korean War was started by the US, when in fact it started when the North invaded the South, and the US came to their assistance. They are taught that we have been harassing the Korean people ever since and are their worst enemies. Ongoing nuclear and missile tests, and military buildups, are viewed with admiration for the leaders' foresight in preparing for self-defense against their perceived enemy. The entire culture has been fabricated on a bed of lies."

"Now what I want to talk about first," said Todd, changing the subject, "is the hackers in China."

He pulled out his iPad with his notes. "Some of what I have here is in the public domain, and other data have been culled by our team in Langley. Shenyang is the capital and largest city of Liaoning Province, as well as the largest city in Northeast China by urban population, with more than eight million inhabitants. A Titan of heavy industry since the 1930s, the city has been diversifying its industry and now has a solid industrial foundation, a good land and air transportation network, abundant natural resources, and a skilled workforce. It is situated only 150 miles from the border with North Korea."

Matt grabbed another Cornish pasty. They were superb.

"The sub-provincial city of Shenyang has direct jurisdiction over nine districts. Launched in 1988 as the Shenyang National New and High-Tech Industrial Development Zone and elevated to a national-zone in 1991, the Hunnan New District, in Southeast Shenyang, south of the Hun River, focuses on electronics and information technology products such as software, computers, network systems, and communications and audio/visual equipment; advanced manufacturing technologies, especially for automobiles, medical equipment; advanced materials and biological and pharmaceutical products. The zone has hosted more than 5,700 enterprises, including seven hundred foreign-invested enterprises. Foreign companies such as General Electric Co., Tyco International, and Mitsubishi Corp. operate in the zone."

"I had no idea," observed Matt, "frightening."

"It gets worse," continued Todd. "It is here that North Korea chose to build their huge workforce of hackers, operating under the guise of software application developers, although some were also based in the Chilbosan Hotel in the Heping District, a North Korean-Chinese joint venture. Shenyang is multiethnic, a place where many foreigners live, especially from Japan and Korea. Korean food, such as rice cakes and cold noodles, is a part of Shenyangers' diet given the sizable ethnic Korean population in the city, and the hackers and their true purpose slip under the radar. Incidentally, North Korea and the US both have consulates in Shenyang's Heping District."

"I can understand the level of concern!" said Matt, "Holy shit!"

"I'll forward this report to you, Matt. We're still figuring out how best to stop these hackers, or at least put them out of operation for a long time. We can't really blame the hackers themselves, but we must send a message to those assholes giving the orders," concluded Todd.

"Now I want to talk about the tunnels again," said Todd, "but maybe we should go for a smoke break first."

They topped up their coffee mugs and went outside.

"How come it's always my cigars?" asked Matt, sarcastically.

"Because you can expense them," quipped Todd.

They talked about anything but the business in hand and Matt took the opportunity to make a quick call to Federica. He heard lots of excited Italians chattering in the background. They were having dinner and Federica sounded as if she'd had one too many glasses of wine, but otherwise sounded fine.

"Ti amo," said Matt before he hung up.

His phone rang a few seconds later, "ti amo," Federica responded and hung up.

They had crossed a line.

Matt and Todd went back to their meeting room.

"The tunnel is still a mystery," said Todd. "It's already longer than previous ones, and now that we have eyes in it, it seems to be narrower than the preceding excavations, so its purpose is unlikely to be for troops."

"Any idea where it's headed?" asked Matt.

"No," said Todd, "that's part of the mystery. It's still headed due south, but no indication of its ultimate destination. We can see power lines, lighting, ventilation and tracks used for carting debris from digging, but that's about it."

"How far is it from the DMZ to Seoul?" asked Matt. "About thirty-five miles," answered Todd. "Why?"

Matt ignored the question, but asked, "Do you have idea yet what the sarin is for?"

Todd gulped and suddenly felt nauseous, but just asked, "When can you travel to Seoul? I can arrange for a company Gulfstream to fly you there, but also want you to check out Shenyang in China. That will need to be a commercial flight, because you'll have to go as a tourist. You can take a commercial flight back to Seoul and use the Gulfstream to travel home."

"I'll need to sort out a few things at home, book my flights to Shenyang then I'll be ready to go in about one week," replied Matt.

"Dinner before you leave?" asked Todd.

"Thanks, but no thanks," was Matt's reply, "I'll eat onboard. But first tell me what's going on with Hassan since the UK incident."

"He's still in hospital being mended," said Todd. "MI6 is sending the bill to Pakistan for that and the escorted flight to Karachi. I wish them good luck with recovering the expense but why should I care?"

They walked outside toward Matt's Learjet. They passed by a beautifully restored Jaguar Mark 2 in British racing green.

"That yours? You got rid of your E-Type?" asked Matt.

"My pride and joy," said Todd. "It's more than fifty years old now but runs like a dream, though I must confess I've spent a fortune on it to get it in this condition."

"She's a beauty," said Matt, "a pity you'll have to replace it with a minivan soon when the baby comes."

"No way," laughed Todd. "I'll find the money somewhere so I can keep her. And no, I didn't get rid of the E-Type. My wife totaled it. I think that was the night I made her pregnant. She doesn't dare to drive the Mark 2."

Matt boarded his airplane and took off after being cleared. As soon as they reached cruising height he warmed up soup, found sandwiches and poured himself a glass of wine. He couldn't help thinking about the sarin and the tunnel. If there was any truth in his wild speculation, the outcome could be catastrophic. He made a mental note to contact his friend Colonel Joe Howard and meet him in Seoul, but he would not mention that to Todd yet. Unbeknown to Talbot, Todd Miller was having similar nightmares about the possible sarin scenario as he drove home, damn near causing an accident as he drove through a stop sign. Finally, Matt slept a little, after a scotch and a cigar, but soon afterwards they landed in Montgomery Field. He drove home and discovered his housekeeper had very thoughtfully prepared him a meal of cold cuts and salad. He devoured it with a large scotch and went to bed.

Chapter 13
La Jolla Again

California, 2017

THE NEXT MORNING MATT called Federica to tell her about his new trip, though of course without too many details. He suggested she stay in Italy for a little longer, but she had apparently been offered a modeling assignment in Vienna for a couple of weeks and it was too lucrative to turn down. He wished her luck but wasn't really focusing. She asked if he was OK and he assured her he was just a little tired but otherwise perfectly relaxed. He felt rather guilty that he couldn't share the truth with her.

He went online with his wonderful new iMac to look at the most convenient flights from Seoul to Shenyang and discovered it was easier than he had imagined. There were four flights per day and they took less than two hours; he booked a return flight with Korean Air, then sent email to Todd to coordinate with the availability of the CIA airplane. He booked his hotels, this time the Grand Hyatt in Seoul and took a risk with the Shangri-La Hotel in Shenyang. Not much of a risk he thought; their hotels were normally superb, and it was just thirty minutes by taxi from Taoxian airport. He had a short-term cash crisis and called Todd's secretary to arrange for an advance. He emailed Colonel Howard in Seoul, and then he was done. The Gulfstream was arriving the next morning but not until late. He called an old friend and invited him out for dinner.

The airplane arrived on time and they took off for Seoul. More kimchi soon he thought, but tucked in to a rather delicious meal of sole, new potatoes and peas. The CIA was improving, he thought, but maybe Todd had had a word with inflight services. It was a rather long flight; the Gulfstream G550 had a range of 6,750 miles and they needed two refueling stops where they also took on fresh food and additional passengers.

Chapter 14
And More Kimchi

Seoul, 2017

MATT'S FLIGHT LANDED at Incheon International Airport on-time where he was met and driven to his hotel. A package was waiting for him containing his favorite handgun, the Kimber, should he need it. He hoped not.

He was escorted to his suite and ordered a light meal from room service then slept after unpacking. He ordered an American breakfast upon waking and called Colonel Howard about lunch then took a taxi to the officers club at the US Army base in Itaewon.

Joe was waiting there to welcome him when he arrived, punctual as usual. They walked to the dining room and it's very attentive Korean waiters and choose a quiet corner where they could talk. Vodka martinis arrived while they perused the menu.

"So what brings you here this time, Matt?" asked Joe.

"As you already know, Joe, I have on occasion helped the CIA with covert work when they needed deniability. I need some advice about a new situation that cropped up recently," said Matt.

"Fire away," said Joe, "but choose your food first. I'm starving. The ribs here are great."

Matt took his advice though he never quite understood that messy way of eating.

"How much do you know about the Korean subway network," asked Talbot.

"Quite a lot actually," responded Howard, "I've been here off and on since they started creating it and gave them lots of advice. Before I joined the military, I was heavily involved at a junior level in the management of the New York subway system."

The ribs arrived and they were indeed delicious. Matt was even more impressed when a waiter appeared with finger bowls so they could clean their hands after eating. They didn't talk much more until the ribs were devoured, then ordered apple pie and ice cream, more martinis and continued.

"First," said Joe, "although you've been here several times, you might appreciate a little background to put everything into perspective."

"Please go ahead," said Matt. "I'll record this if you don't mind."

"OK," continued Joe, "Itaewon itself refers to an area surrounding Itaewon-dong, Yongsan-gu, in Seoul. It's served by Seoul Subway Line 6 via Itaewon, Noksapyeong and Hanganjin stations. About 20,000 people live in the district and it's a popular area for local residents, tourists and US military personnel.

As you know, many restaurants serving international dishes are found in the area including cuisine from India, Pakistan, Turkey, Thailand, Germany, Spain, Italy, England, France and Mexico; foods not widely available in other parts of Korea.

Major hotels, such as yours, are here, as well as the dozens of shops and services aimed at tourists. High-quality leather products can be found at reasonable prices (though haggling is expected) beside traditional Korean souvenirs. Counterfeit goods and clothing are ubiquitous but of varying quality. Some genuine goods, produced in Korea for the international market, and some authentic imports can also be found. Itaewon is known for its tailors producing custom-made suits and shirts. Be sure to order some before you leave. They can normally deliver to your hotel within two days.

There is a portion of Itaewon known as "Hooker Hill." Although the stereotype is of only American servicemen visiting, this area is well known among men visiting from other countries.

Yongsan District sits to the north of the Han River under the shadow of Seoul Tower, in the center of Seoul. It's home to roughly 250,000 people and is divided into twenty dong, or neighborhoods. The District is home to Yongsan Garrison, a large US military base in the heart of Seoul. 28,500 soldiers, sailors, airmen and marines are stationed there.

And now back to your original question about the subway system: The Seoul Metropolitan Subway has been described as the world's longest multi-operator metro system by route length, and was rated as one of the world's best subway systems by CNN. It's notable for its cleanliness and ease-of-use, with advanced technology such as 4G LTE, Wi-Fi, DMB, and WiBro accessible in all stations and moving subway cars. Most trains have digital TV screens, and all of them have air-conditioning and climate-controlled seats, automatically heated during the winter.

All lines use the T-money smart payment system using RFID and NFC technology for automatic payment by T-money smart cards, smartphones, or credit cards and one can transfer to any other lines in the system for free. Seoul subway is the world's only metro system to use full-color LCD screens at all stations to display real-time subway arrival times, also available on apps for smartphones. All directional signs in the system are written in Korean, English and Hanja.

Opening of the system began in 1974 when Line 1 connecting Seongbuk to Incheon and Suwon was declared ready for use, and regular updates to the network have taken place ever since, with scheduled additions currently planned through 2020. 2006 saw the opening of Line 6, providing service to and from Itaewon, close to the US Army base, the notorious Hamilton Hotel, markets and various embassies."

Matt turned off the record function on his iPhone and asked, "thanks a million, Joe; one question out of curiosity. You mentioned Line 6 runs very close to the army base. Is access provided directly into the system from the base?"

"Funny you should ask," replied Joe, "about one year ago, we provided that access for a privileged few. One can use an access card and walk right into the subway system. I can take you over there for a look, if you'd like."

Matt's palms started to sweat as he said, "yes please, Joe."

Joe Howard signed the bill and they walked to the subway access entrance inside one the larger buildings inside the base. Matt noticed a CCTV camera pointing at the door. Joe swiped a magnetic card and they walked down a few steps, opened a second door, and entered the subway proper. Matt asked if he could take a few photos.

Joe asked, "Why all this interest in subways and our access point?"

"Just my natural curiosity," Matt lied, "I've never used the Seoul subways and was interested in how far they've come."

"I need to get back to work," said Joe, "I'll escort you out."

They shook hands outside the base and Matt took a cab back to his hotel. He wrote a terse email to Todd, attached the recording and his photos, and asked him to call. It took him only ten minutes.

"What was all this about?" asked Todd. Matt explained he had had lunch with his old friend Colonel Howard and had quizzed him about the subway system and was surprised to discover there was an access point right inside the army base.

"That entrance must be a well-kept secret," said Todd, "I knew nothing about it."

"Now imagine if someone could get into the subway system and release gas that could travel into the base!" supposed Matt, "food for thought. Is there any way the guys up north could know about the workings of the subway system and the secret entrance?"

"I'd never say it's impossible," Todd replied, "I'm going to stir up the shit in Langley. Thanks for the initiative, Matt. Now get your ass over to our tunnel guys to see firsthand what the fuck is going on." He hung up, angrily.

Chapter 15
Pyongyang

North Korea, 2017

AN EMERGENCY MEETING had been convened in Pyongyang between the Reconnaissance General Bureau (RGB), the main intelligence service, and Office 225, responsible for operations in South Korea. It was one of many such gatherings over the last several weeks. Kim Jong-un did not typically attend such meetings, preferring to receive a summation afterward, when he would frequently interject his wishes.

The first item on the agenda was sarin gas. It's procurement in Syria had proved challenging, not because of availability, but rather the difficulty of arranging funds given the sanctions imposed by the US following the Sony hacking episode. Ultimately funding had been arranged via sympathetic parties in Baghdad. Transporting the gas turned out to be remarkably straightforward. Given the binary characteristics of the weapon it was safe to transport so long as the two precursors were kept apart. The canisters were packed securely and flown to Pyongyang. They were now stored in a secure location.

The main subject of discussion was the status of tunneling that was taking longer than anticipated. When the tunnel project was conceived, it had been decided to procure a tunnel boring machine, but after investigation that approach had been abandoned. The first obstacle encountered was that such huge pieces of machinery were not in common use around the world, and if North Korea's purchase of such a device were to have become known, eyebrows would have been raised in all the wrong places. The second problem was the noise such machines produced, that would certainly have been detected. Major changes in direction were made. The scope of the project, originally intended to allow thousands of troops to enter South Korea, was scaled back. The tunnel was being dug using manual labor, albeit with the most modern and quietest tools available. The tunnel was deeper and narrower than originally planned and sophisticated strengthening materials were used to shore up the excavation and to carry power lines and air-conditioning. Tracks were laid to allow small electrically powered carts to remove debris, and to transport the laborers when they changed shifts. Small tributary rooms were constructed to provide eating and toilet facilities.

But the most significant change was to tunnel all the way to Seoul and break into the subway system. The same electric carts would be used to transport sarin gas to the South Korean capital.

BM Min, responsible for the tunnel project, was in the hot seat, and as usual he was pummeled with terse questions.

"What can be done to speed up the tunneling?" asked JW Hyung.

BM stood his ground, "nothing," he replied, "we're running three shifts per day; we feed the men well and weed out anyone not pulling his weight. We've often encountered granite that slows us down."

"Any indication of detection?" JW asked.

"None whatsoever," replied BM, "we are careful to minimize the noise generated."

The questions continued ad nauseam.

It was KC Park's turn for the hot seat.

"Anything to report?" asked JW.

"Yes, I may have significant news," said KC smiling. "As you know, I've had a mole inside the US Army base in Itaewon for a while now, posing as a cleaner. He noticed a strange door inside one of the buildings. It has no sign but has a magnetic stripe reader to gain entry. The strange thing is, given the layout of the building, it's not physically possible for there to be a room on the other side. It can only lead downward. He's seen a few senior personnel go through the entrance but they don't return, at least not while he was watching. He has to be careful."

"Interesting," said JW, "do you think it may be an entrance to the subway?"

"The thought passed through my mind," replied KC.

"Find out more," ordered JW. "We don't want to risk discovery, but if it is indeed a subway shortcut that's very valuable information for us. It may provide a more effective method of getting gas into the base."

Chapter 16
Langley Again

Virginia, 2017

TODD MILLER WAS STILL extremely angry that it had taken an outside contractor to figure out what was probably going down in Korea. Not the CIA, not the NSA, but Matt Talbot. He was certainly not upset with Matt, though a little jealous. He felt he had enough information to escalate this to Director John Peel. He relayed his fears, to add to the regular reports that Peel had already seen.

"What do you need?" Peel asked.

"I already have a small team in South Korea spying on the North's tunnel operation, as you know. As far as we know, they have no idea we're onto them. Talbot is over there right now, and he'll be figuring out how we might enter the tunnel when the time is right, and the gas is on its way, if our speculation is correct. We'll need to get hazmat suits and sarin gas expertise in place over there," said Miller.

"That's all well and good," said Peel, "but as good as Talbot is, he's no mining expert, nor does he have much knowledge of nerve gases."

"I'm well aware of that sir, but I don't intend to use him for the insertion. We have the resources to effect that. I want Talbot to assess the situation first; he has extremely good intuition. After that, he'll travel to Shenyang to look at the lay of the land. I want him to assemble a team to disable the North's hacking team, as you will have seen from my report."

"Good thinking," agreed Peel. "It's OK to have CIA people charging about in South Korea but if things go pear-shaped in Shenyang we need deniability."

"I've got some ideas about how to disguise the true identity of Matt's team when we're ready," continued Miller.

The meeting was over, but as Todd prepared to leave, he said, "by the way, director, it was Talbot who put two and two together about what's probably going on in Korea."

"We should hire him," said Peel, glaring at Miller, "why the fuck did nobody here come up with that?"

Chapter 17
The White House

Washington DC, 2017

As soon as Peel's door was closed, he placed a call to Secretary of State William Mitchell to brief him, who in turn briefed Melissa Osborne, the National Security Adviser.

Within the hour President Clinton was fully aware; she had seen snippets of the situation in her daily briefings but this was obviously becoming very serious now, far beyond the saber-rattling they had become accustomed to. She called an emergency meeting with Mitchell, Osborne and General Bertrand Rushmore, Chairman of the Joint Chiefs of Staff.

"General," President Clinton started, "what is the current disposition of the 7th Fleet?"

The 7th Fleet is the largest of the forward-deployed US fleets, consisting of sixty to seventy ships, three hundred aircraft and forty thousand Navy and Marine Corps personnel. One of their three assignments is the defense of the Korean Peninsula.

"Madam President," replied the general, "some of the fleet and personnel are currently positioned in Yokosuka, with the balance deployed off South Korea."

"We need the resources in Japan to be ready to move at a moment's notice, to join in a huge demonstration of force in conjunction with South Korea off the Korean Peninsula," stated Clinton.

"Of course, Madam President. May I ask what's going on?"

President Clinton briefed him.

"Oh my God," was all he could say.

"Our suspicions should not go farther than these four walls until we have more evidence," said Clinton, "Melissa, please remain when the others leave."

When Mitchell and the general had left, President Clinton requested that Melissa liaise with John Peel and contact the CDC for help with sarin experts, hazmat suits and whatever other equipment Peel might need, to be rushed out to Seoul as quickly as possible.[17] Hillary called Park Geun-hye, president of South Korea since 2013, to inform her of their suspicions and assure her that they had deployed multiple resources, but with necessary caution for now. President Park assured her ally of her full cooperation.

---

17   CDC: Centers for Disease Control and Prevention.

Chapter 18
The Tunnel

Seoul, Korea, 2017

JACK MATHIS, HEAD OF THE CIA's Seoul-based office, gave Talbot a ride to the heavily guarded high-tech trailer acting as the command center for the tunnel monitoring operation. His first order of business was to review recordings made of the tunnel excavation by the optical and audio sensors established over the last few weeks. Talbot marveled at the clarity of the recordings as he randomly skimmed through the records. He could clearly see laborers laying tracks for electric carts, and as the optics swiveled he could see them excavating at the face, welding steel supports, laying electric cables and installing lighting and air-conditioning ducts. After a while, something caught his attention as he went back and forth through the recordings. He had seen the men transporting what looked like acetylene gas cylinders for welding, but he could also see smaller cylinders being moved. The audio recordings, mostly of no use, had picked up a couple of the guys shouting 'careful' as they placed the cylinders into receptacles cut into niches in the tunnel walls. As he looked again at other recordings, he figured out the small cylinders were being progressively moved south as the tunnel became longer. Talbot called Jack Mathis over and pointed out his observations of the cylinders.

"Notice anything strange?" He asked.

"No," said Mathis, "I assumed they are oxyacetylene for welding."

"They never get used," observed Talbot, "they just get moved."

He called over one the CDC experts who had flown in the previous day and asked his opinion. He said, in view of the calls for caution and the size of the cylinders, they could hold volatile contents, confirming Talbot's suspicions.

"If they contain sarin," asked Talbot, "how could they be deployed?"

"First the cylinders, or their contents, would have to be moved up to the level of the target," replied Dr. March, "sarin vapor is heavier than air. If the gas was activated in the tunnel, it would simply sink to low-lying areas but not disperse upward."

Interesting, thought Talbot. This triggered another thought in Matt's mind and he went back to reviewing the recordings. His suspicions were confirmed when he saw lengths of flexible hose and what could be small electric pumps stored with the gas cylinders. He quizzed the doctor a little longer and discovered that sarin, normally in liquid form, evaporates quickly, presenting an immediate but short-lived threat. It could be used to contaminate either water or food supplies. The doctor confirmed that the sarin gas could indeed be pumped up to a higher elevation by setting up a pressure differential.

"Did you know any of this?" Talbot asked Mathis.

"No, I did not," he replied.

Matt was furious with this little cocksucker but did not speak his mind yet. It was not his place to do so.

Talbot asked Mathis to go over the preliminary plan to enter the tunnel and incapacitate it. Mathis called over the head tunnel guy, Marty Lee.

"Marty and his team will be drilling a man-size hole where we have our first listening post, close to but not visible to the DMZ," said Mathis.

"How quiet will that process be?" asked Talbot.

Lee replied, "we'll be as quiet as possible," he said, "but it will start to get very noisy as we get close to breaking through the roof of the tunnel."

"Then what?" asked Talbot. "We plan to lower two guys in hazmat suits down into the tunnel to disable the power lines," said Mathis, "then return to the surface."

"Then what?" Talbot asked.

"We fully expect the laborers to start leaving the tunnel since they will only be able to see using flashlights, they'll have no power for their tools, and fresh air will have stopped flowing. After that we'll lower charges to collapse the tunnel," said Mathis.

"How do you think the Koreans will react when they hear you drilling?" asked Talbot.

Mathis said nothing.

"If I were in their place," said Talbot angrily, "I'd send troops down the tunnel and take out your guys. And what about the sarin?"

"As soon as we figure out where it is, we plan to send more guys with hazmat suits down into the tunnel to bring it out, and then safely dispose of it. In light of your earlier discussion with Dr. March we may need to revisit that part of the plan."

Talbot lost his cool.

"You're an idiot," he said loudly to Mathis.

The trailer went very, very quiet.

"What did you call me?" said an astounded Mathis, "you don't even work for the CIA and you come in here criticizing an approved plan."

"I withdraw my remark," said Talbot, "you're a fucking idiot."

Talbot punched him as hard as he could on his jaw. The other inhabitants of the trailer either laughed, cheered, or both. Mathis lay on the floor, unconscious. Talbot nursed his sore knuckles then walked over, extracted the car keys from Mathis' pocket and left.

He excused himself, went outside, and called Todd Miller.

Matt was not known for his subtlety and his opening remark was, "Jack Mathis is not worth Jack shit."

He explained to Todd what he had learned over the last few hours and Miller listened patiently until the end.

"He used the word 'assumed' at least twice," said Talbot angrily, "in my opinion, assumption is the mother of fuck-up, and it's not in my vocabulary. I think you'd better get your ass over here, as you said to me on more than one occasion. It's not my place to chastise or give orders. Oh, and by the way, Mathis needs medical attention. I hit him."

"Oh my God, how do I explain that?" said Miller.

"Who approved the stupid plan?" asked Talbot.

"I did," Miller replied, "but now you've updated me, it's obviously flawed."

"The plan is a load of bollocks," Matt said.

"Can you say that again in American English?" asked Todd.

"It's shit. It's crap. It won't work, OK?" said Matt, "are you OK? This is not the normal you."

"Well," said Miller, "my boss recently ripped me a new one, and Wendy had a miscarriage. Other than that I'm fine."

"I'm so sorry to hear that," Matt replied, "what a mess. I know how much you were both looking forward to the baby."

"Don't worry, Matt," said Todd, "Wendy's sister is flying in so I can focus more on my job and I will indeed get my ass over there, as you so tactfully suggested."

"How do you think we should change the plan?" asked Todd.

"To my mind it's very simple," said Matt, "we do indeed bore a larger hole close the DMZ, almost but not quite breaching the tunnel. But we don't need people down there. We drop a sizable charge, big enough to collapse the tunnel and cut the power, air and communications. If, by that time, military are present, that's too bad. Then we drill more holes going southwards and drop more charges and progressively collapse the entire structure, but we stop before we get to the suspected storage place for the sarin cylinders, hoses and pumps. We don't need to worry about drilling noise; anyone still in the tunnel won't be able to communicate."

"What about the laborers down there?" asked Todd.

"They never should have been there in the first place," said Matt, "they are in direct violation of the 1953 armistice agreement. They die of suffocation or starvation. The sarin gas has a short life and will cause no harm."

"Sounds like a workable plan," said Todd, "though I'll have to pass it by the Director, of course, then I'll be over there. I'll sort out the Mathis mess, and clearly I need another head of station for Seoul. What's your plan now?"

"I'm going to drive back to my hotel, check out and fly to Shenyang," said Matt.

They hung up.

In fact Matt drove to the CIA offices first, returned the Toyota Land Cruiser he had purloined, and his Kimber, then caught a cab to his hotel. Before he checked out he dashed off a quick email to Todd, suggesting he do two more things: have the pilot holes they had drilled for tunnel observation blocked off after they were no longer needed, just in case, and have the subway entrance from the Itaewon base hermetically sealed. This was all about the small but important details. Thinking of which, Matt wondered how on earth the Koreans intended to pump the sarin gas to their target without detection.

Chapter 19
The Pyongyang Dilemma

North Korea, 2017

BY COINCIDENCE, the same dilemma was being discussed further north. JW Hyung was not a happy man. He turned to KS Mac, the sarin expert, who was perspiring heavily.

"I hear you have news," Hyung stated.

"Yes, I have disturbing news," Mac stuttered, "after exploring all possibilities we have concluded it's impossible to pump the sarin gas to our target without detection. There is no way we can lay the gas pipeline without arousing suspicion. We will get caught and the entire operation will be for naught."

"What do you mean?" asked Hyung, "you have only just reached this conclusion, so late in the game?"

Mac was breathing heavily now as he sputtered his answer, "we explored all possibilities," he said, his voice trailing off.

JW called the guards over to escort Mac from the room. He was never seen again. Now Hyung turned to HS Kim who had reported to Mac, and had recently shown great initiative on a number of occasions.

"Kim," Hyung asked, "have you given recent thought to the sarin problem since this was discovered?"

"Yes, sir, I have. We'll have to have men carry the cylinders into the subway from the tunnel. They are not large or heavy and can be easily disguised until we begin the mixing process."

"Those men will die," stated Hyung, unnecessarily.

"They can carry protective suits with them and put them on just before releasing the gas. The suits we have are not true hazmat suits but they should reassure the wearers while they carry out their duty. They will die for the cause," Kim stated off-handedly.

"Very well," said Hyung, "proceed with detailed planning and report to me in future."

Hyung turned to KC Park and stated, "that subway entrance from the army base is now of vital importance, given it's the only way of delivering sarin to the American troops."

"I realize that, sir," Park replied, "we'll have to figure out a plan to carry it up to the base, rather than pumping it from below."

Hyung called the meeting to a close, left the room, and issued orders for the execution of the disgraced Mac.

Chapter 20
Visiting Shenyang

China, 2017

TALBOT WAS TRAVELING as a tourist. He showed his Chinese visa, checked in on Korean Air at Incheon and tried to relax for his short flight. It was uneventful. After landing at Taoxian airport, he was appalled at the smog and pollution. He learned later that Shenyang was the most polluted city in all of China, given the heavy industry and coal mining. Why had no one warned him of this? For the actual operation, they could not describe themselves as tourists. Why the fuck would a tourist come to this hell hole? He caught a taxi to the Shangri-La hotel on Qingnian Avenue and went to the coffee shop for a light meal and a glass of the local wine, which he did not enjoy. But it did make him sleepy which is what he needed. He went to his room and bathed his sore knuckles again, smiling at the memory. What a jerk that guy Mathis was, he thought. He had bought a bottle of scotch in the duty-free shop in Incheon and he poured a couple of shots before calling Federica. It had only been a few days but it seemed like weeks. He got through to her cellphone on the first try and she was very happy to hear from him. She was staying at the magnificent Hotel Palais Schwarzenberg in Vienna, a hotel that he remembered dearly and he wished he could change places or better still, be there with her, but that was not to be. He enjoyed just talking about simple things, his flight to Shenyang, and after a few days, flying back to California where they would meet again. He took a shower and slept.

He was rudely awakened soon afterward by a knock at the door. He turned on the bedside light and looked through the peephole in the door.

"Yes?" he asked.

"Room service," was the reply.

"I ordered nothing," he answered, half asleep.

"A welcome gift from the hotel management," was the reply.

Talbot looked through the peephole again. The guy was wearing a hotel uniform and was Chinese. He opened the door, but was immediately alert when the guy locked the door behind him as he wheeled in a trolley with fruit and a half bottle of wine. The 'waiter' flashed a CIA badge and asked Talbot to get dressed and go with him to the CIA office in the nearby consulate building.

"Now why in the world would I do that?" asked Talbot, "I'm an American tourist and you're a ridiculous impostor."

CS Lee, as he called himself, pulled a gun. Talbot twisted it from his grip, breaking one of his fingers in the process, then removed the magazine and threw both the gun and the magazine across the room.

"Who the fuck gave you these instructions?" asked a very angry Talbot.

"I received the order from Seoul," said Lee, gasping in pain.

"Let me guess, Jack Mathis?"

"Yes," said Lee, "he was calling from his doctor's treatment room. He has a broken jaw and the doctor had just finished wiring it up."

"Do you know the name Todd Miller?" asked Talbot.

"Of course," responded Lee, "our operations officer."

"I'm calling him right now," said Talbot as he picked up his cellphone.

Todd was in flight to Seoul and Matt related the most recent episode. Todd sighed and asked whether Lee had been hurt.

"Only slightly," said Matt, "he just needs a finger splint."

"When we're done please pass your phone to Lee. Meanwhile I'll call ahead to Seoul and have Mathis put in custody. I have his replacement traveling with me."

Miller spoke to Lee briefly; Lee gave his apology to Talbot who reciprocated then left to drive to a clinic, but not before Talbot handed his gun back to him. Matt went back to bed. Another day in paradise.

Talbot was slightly late starting the following morning after a restless night, but went down to the coffee shop and ordered a bowl of congee and tea. He took a taxi to the Chilbosan Hotel on Shiyiwei Road and looked at the board listing companies having offices there. He spotted three with names sounding like software businesses, and one called Cybertek stood out. He took the elevator up to the third floor and entered the lobby, approaching the receptionist. He explained he was a director of a video games company based in Silicon Valley in California and he was looking to outsource some of their development work, producing a fake business card he had had printed before he left Seoul. The receptionist asked him to take a seat and made a call. Talbot looked around the nicely furnished lobby, noticing three security cameras. Five minutes later a smartly dressed guy emerged from behind a locked door and introduced himself simply as Choe. His business card described him as the General Manager. He was very civil, but explained that this was a very small office with only a handful of key managers and no development work was done here. Talbot found this very difficult to believe, since it was quite obvious from the notice board in the lobby that there must be at least fifty people working here. He asked Choe if he could recommend another company here in Shenyang that might be able to help him, but nothing was forthcoming. Feeling rather frustrated but hardly surprised, Talbot thanked him and left. On the way to the elevator he noticed several unmarked doors, solidifying his suspicion of the number of people working here for Cybertek. Given the suspected scope of the hacking operation, there must be another Cybertek office.

Back in the lobby, Matt walked to the reception desk and asked for the concierge's help in trying to locate the main office. He was very helpful, and in addition to the rooms here in the hotel, he found another address in an office block nearby. Matt thanked him and leaving a generous tip, walked toward the hotel entrance.

The concierge called Choe as he had been instructed, to warn him. Choe in turn called Jeong, the GM of the primary office, to tell him to expect a visitor inquiring about offshore development work. Once outside, Talbot took a few photographs of the hotel with his iPhone. To a casual observer he would have looked like any other visitor. He noted that the hotel had sixteen floors and a flat roof. He took more photographs.

Talbot took the short walk to Cybertek's main office. Once again, after he had asked directions for the office from the building's concierge, there was a nicely furnished reception area, complete with a pretty girl behind the desk, flanked by security cameras. Talbot repeated his story and was soon greeted by Mr. Jeong. Jeong gave a slightly different response almost too quickly, as if it had been rehearsed. He stated very politely that they did not have the resources to take on additional work at the moment since their calendar was completely full for at least two years. Talbot asked about the nature of the work in process, but Jeong was very evasive and looked increasingly nervous. Again, as he left the building, Talbot took a few photographs of the building and its surroundings.

Matt strolled a little, looking for an outdoor café where he could sit and call Todd Miller. He passed by an Apple Store, one of two in Shenyang, beautifully designed as always, rather incongruous given the surroundings. Then he found his café, ordered a disgusting coffee sweetened with evaporated milk, and placed his call. Miller was in Seoul by now, and Matt related what had transpired.

"All is not lost, Matt," he said, "we should be able to cross-check the addresses of the buildings you visited with the traces we made of their IP addresses, so at least we'll have confirmation of their operating bases."

"We must remember also that the bastards most likely have my face recorded as a visitor to both buildings," noted Matt.

"I think you're done there, Matt," said Todd, "let's meet here in

Seoul before you fly back to the US." Just to be on the safe side, Matt mailed the photographs to Todd's iPad.

Matt returned to his hotel, checked out and took a cab to the airport.

Chapter 21
Back to the Garlic Eaters

Seoul, 2017

TALBOT LANDED AGAIN at his second home, Incheon airport, where a CIA car was waiting to drive him to the embassy to meet Miller. They walked to a secure meeting room where Miller introduced the new Seoul station head, Dirk Potter.

"You've met before," said Todd, "Dirk was working the Pakistan operation with me."

"Yes, I remember you," said Talbot.

"Dirk has done some excellent work for us recently," said Todd, "and he's earned this posting."

"Do I need a flak jacket?" asked Potter, smiling.

"No, I only hurt assholes or people who were given orders by assholes," said Matt, also smiling, "which reminds me, what's happened to Mathis?"

"Oh, he has a meaningless desk job in Langley now. His jaw has been put out of joint in more ways than one," said Todd.

Matt just laughed.

"By the way, Matt," Todd continued, "you'll meet Lee again later, but don't worry, he bears no grudge. He's as happy as anyone to see the back of Mathis."

"Hungry?" asked Todd. "All I can offer at this time of the day is doughnuts."

"I'll pass," said Matt.

"We've discussed the revised tunnel plan you related to me in depth, Matt," said Todd, "we've refined it a little but not significantly, I passed it by Director Peel and he's on board. I also filled him in on Mathis. I seem to be in his good books again for now."

"What part of the plan changed?" asked Matt.

"We will not seal the Itaewon entrance to the subway yet," said Todd, "one of the Korean cleaners seems to be taking an inordinate amount of interest in the door. We've seen him on the surveillance recordings. We may have a mole. We want to wait and learn more. But the main thing we need to talk about right now is Shenyang. We want you to pull a team together to penetrate those two facilities and wreck their hacking operation."

"Surely no assassinations in China!" Matt exclaimed.

"No," said Todd, "far more subtle. We'll give you the tools to steal and purge the data on their network, servers and workstations, both in Shenyang and Pyongyang, then fry all the equipment remotely. We've been at this game long enough to figure out how to put them out of operation for a very long time."

"How do we hide the countries of origin of my team members?" asked Matt, "there could be serious repercussions, and not just by the North Koreans."

"We want no violence unless it's unavoidable," said Todd, "you need to find team members who speak fluent Russian, and you'll be armed with Russian weapons. You'll need to leave one or two firearms behind. We want to confuse the crap out of them. You'll enter and leave the country as tourists and carry nothing for the actual operation that could be used to trace you to your origins. You'll wear gloves. No fingerprints. Director Peel has brought the proposed operation to the attention of the administration and has their tacit approval, pending a detailed plan. You'll be paid the usual fees and there will be a generous bonus on completion assuming all goes well, all tax-free. Time is of the essence, Matt. What say you?"

"First, we cannot visit as tourists. No one warned me about the pollution. We'll have to act as businessmen looking for investment opportunities. I need a little time to digest this, Todd," he said, "but right now I need to digest something else, and not Chinese or kimchi."

Todd laughed, "how about a good steak?" he asked.

Lee had just flown in from Shenyang and joined them briefly.

Talbot walked toward him and held out his right hand, but Lee didn't immediately offer his, saying, "please be gentle. My finger is still recovering!"

They smiled and shook hands, gently.

"I sympathize with your situation," said Matt, "what did you do wrong to end up in a place like Shenyang?"

"I was asked to go there on a two-year assignment since I'm single and can speak fluent Mandarin and Korean, with a promise of a more desirable location afterward," Lee replied.

"Good luck!" said Matt.

Todd requested a car to be brought round and took Matt to an excellent steakhouse he had recently discovered. Matt was deep in thought. They were given an excellent table in the restaurant where Todd had befriended the maître d'. They ordered vodka martinis. Matt ordered a medium-rare filet mignon with French fries and a mixed salad; Todd ordered lamb chops, new potatoes, and fresh vegetables, for a change, and a bottle of Beaujolais.

"How's Wendy now?" asked Matt.

"OK under the circumstances I suppose," Todd answered, "I'm not exactly her favorite guy after announcing this trip on top of her recent trauma. And her doctor told her the miscarriage was probably the result of stress. I interpreted that to mean it was related to worrying about me and my job."

Matt was silent.

"And how's Federica?" asked Todd.

"Living a life of luxury at the moment, in Vienna," said Matt, "last time we spoke she had just been to listen to the Vienna Boys Choir and thoroughly enjoyed it. Fortunately she has little idea about my strange life, only that I conduct business with the CIA. I'm seriously thinking about asking her to move in with me when we're both back there."

"So soon after Jessica?" asked Todd, "knowing your history, you must have a weapon of mass seduction."

Matt laughed, "My weak spot for smart beautiful ladies I suppose, and anyway she spends most of her time with me whenever we're both in town."

They didn't talk too much about the business in hand. Matt needed more time to process what he needed to do to get his team convinced and onboard. This was not exactly the kind of operation they were used to. They finished the meal with coffee and port wine then called it quits. Todd picked up the check and called his driver to take them to their respective hotels. On the way, he told Matt the Gulfstream would be ready for him in the morning but not to be late. The pilot had other passengers.

To his surprise, Talbot slept well that night. He surfaced early, ate an American breakfast in the hotel, called the Gulfstream pilot, checked out and took a cab. As soon as they went wheels-up he checked email, thanked Todd for his hospitality and reminded him to send more expense advances, then sent his best to Federica who had just been to see the Lipizzan horses perform in Vienna. The rest could wait until he reached home. He ordered a scotch from the very attentive flight attendant and found a favorite old movie to watch on Netflix on his iPad. He fell asleep and did not wake again until they landed to take on fuel and food. He ordered a beef stroganoff and a glass of wine then caught up with the news on CNN while enjoying a cigar. The attendant frowned but turned a blind eye and fetched him another drink. Time went slowly, but by the time they landed at Montgomery Field he knew exactly who he wanted on his team.

Chapter 22
Home Again

La Jolla, 2017

MATT DROVE BACK to La Jolla Farms to find a beautifully clean home, thanks to Maria, and was welcomed by a very enthusiastic Winston. He ignored the letters for now. Nothing of importance since most of his bills were paid online. He made a ham and cheese Panini and poured a glass of wine, then watched TV for a short while before retiring to his own bed, finally. He slept smelling Federica's fragrance that never seemed to go away.

He awoke, showered, went to his Gaggia to craft an espresso and made toast and scrambled eggs, and then sat in front of his iMac to compile his list.

First was Mark Smyth, his ex-SAS colleague who spoke fluent Russian, and was probably itching for action. Next was Peter Brennan, also retired from the SAS. Next were two descendants of Gurkhas, who had served in the British Army. Talbot had first come to know Ganju Lama and Bhanbhagta Guyung (known as Ganja and Bang Bang to their friends) when he was introduced to their fathers at an award ceremony in the UK, and had grown to trust them and their skills completely. Ganju's father had been part of the highly successful SAS raid on the besieged Iranian Embassy in London in 1980, during which the SAS rescued all but one of the remaining hostages and killed five of the six terrorists. Next he left a message for Susan Vierra, though after much deliberation Matt had decided she was not appropriate to join this new operation. She possessed skills second to none in explosives, but her talents would hopefully not be needed in Shenyang, though he wanted to talk to her to assure her she was not forgotten. Last but by no means least he made a note of Lloyd Morris' name. Lloyd was known as their WMD, their weapon of mass destruction.

He started making calls but unlike before when they had relied on covert email, asked them to respond using their secure iPhones; a much safer procedure. That done he went through his snail mail but there was nothing of significance other than a demand for jury duty and another demand from the IRS for unpaid taxes. He called his tax accountant first and asked her to quash that bullshit. The IRS never understood why he enjoyed such a lavish lifestyle while paying minimal taxes, but Marie knew exactly how to deal with them, which is why he had hired her. After all, much of his income, aside from his inheritance, came from government-approved tax-free dollars. He referred the local court to Todd Miller's secretary via email who he trusted would take care of that unnecessary distraction.

It was lunch time. He drove alone to his favorite locally owned French restaurant, Le Bistro, where he was welcomed by the owners, a chef and waitress partnership who served him an exquisite but light meal of sand dabs with potato croquettes and fresh vegetables, followed by a soufflé.

Federica was arriving the next day but before that he needed to think more about how they were going to execute the Shenyang operation. He reviewed the photographs he had taken of the two target buildings in Shenyang and ideas started to form in his mind. Winston was getting restless; he let him outside to perform his urinary gymnastics then took him for a walk. Calls started to come in but he ignored them until he returned home. He needed more time to think about his plan.

Mark Smyth had returned his call first and wanted to know more. He was totally onboard after Matt's brief description. He was at home in Hereford and not doing much of anything.

Matt was not particularly hungry but prepared a light dinner, poured a drink and tried to clear his fuddled brain as he instructed

Siri to find him an old Sean Connery movie. He paused the recording and moved to the bedroom to continue watching after setting a wake-up call on his Watch for the morning.

Federica was arriving on Alitalia after changing flights in Rome. He drove to Lindbergh Field to welcome her and drove home. She looked devastating as usual but despite the pleasures and comfort of a first class flight was rather tired. She apologized, took a shower on reaching Matt's home and went straight to bed. Matt took advantage of the situation and caught up with calls from his colleagues until she reappeared, much refreshed, wearing a T-shirt and nothing else. Time for a late lunch and she prepared pasta, something she had not enjoyed for a while. Matt did not consider it politic to mention that he had already had his fill of garlic over the last few days but consumed it with enthusiasm seeing the glint in her eyes. They passed on desert and moved to the bedroom to celebrate their reunion, then slept for a short while. When they awoke Matt asked whether she would like to move into his home.

She considered that for about one minute, but after reaching for his crotch again and feeling his response said, "yes, that would be a wonderful idea. I can't remember the last time I slept in my own house anyway."

"But I have to tell you, darling, that I have to travel to Asia again soon. Before that I need to join a few colleagues over in Virginia," said Matt.

"It's OK, Matt," she replied, "I have lots to do. I have to unpack, move in my clothes and stuff, and rent out my townhouse."

"Now you're talking," said Matt, and they made love again after her more insistent manipulations of his lower regions.

Federica slept again afterward. Matt took a shower and went back to his office to work the phone.

Peter Brennan had called him from Berlin where he was consulting to a security company but was bored to death and was an easy sell. Ganja and Bang Bang conference-called from Paris where they had been working with the DGSE in the aftermath of another ISIS attack.[18] Lloyd Morris was en-route to his home in

---

18   DGSE: France's General Directorate for External Security. ISIS: Islamic State

Wales and was ready for action. In short, Matt's timing was perfect and the team he wanted was available, and they had all worked together before, most of them in the Abbottābad operation earlier in the year. But he did return Susan's call and tactfully explained why she would not be a part of this particular exercise. She sounded disappointed but understood.

---

of Iraq and Syria.

Chapter 23
CIA Headquarters

Langley, Virginia, 2017

TODD MILLER HAD RETURNED to Langley. He and Matt had agreed on a provisional plan for taking out the hacking network, and now they needed to fly Matt's team in to Langley for briefing and familiarization with the Russian equipment obtained by Nick Bailey, an armorer with the CIA. Todd's secretary had scoured the local hotels for available rooms and meeting facilities but the usual hotels used by CIA visitors were all fully booked and the only venue she could confirm was the Hyatt Regency in Bethesda. Todd was not amused at the cost but had no choice. When the dates were confirmed he would have a team sent over to ensure the meeting facilities were bug-free and secure. The good news was, the hotel was less than four miles from CIA HQ when the time arrived for firearms practice in the range.

Nick Bailey, one of the Langley armorers, had been working hard to identify, acquire and evaluate weapons currently in use by Russia's armed forces and police. The PK is a 7.62mm general-purpose machine gun designed in the Soviet Union and currently in production in Russia. The original PK weapon was introduced in 1961, and then the improved PKM in 1969, to replace the SGM and RP-46 machine guns in Soviet service. The PKM remains in use as a frontline infantry and vehicle-mounted weapon with Russia's armed forces. The PK has been exported extensively and produced in several countries under license. The original PK was a development of Kalashnikov's AK47 automatic rifle design, firing the

7.62x54mm Eastern Bloc standard ammunition originally from the Mosin-Nagant. This was the rifle chosen for the Shenyang operation.

Next was the pistol. The Makarov pistol or PM (Pistolet Makarova), is a Russian semiautomatic pistol. Under the project leadership of Fyodorovich Makarov, it became the Soviet Union's standard military and police sidearm in 1951 and is still in use today. Rather than building a pistol to an existing cartridge in the Soviet inventory, Nikolai Makarov took up the German wartime Walther 'Ultra' design, fundamentally an enlarged Walther PP, using the 9x18mm Makarov cartridge designed by B.V. Semin in 1946. In 2013, the PM was formally replaced by the Yarygin PYa pistol in Russian deployment, although large numbers of PMs were still in Russian military and police service, and were coincidentally standard-issue pistols for North Korean use. The PM was the obvious choice.

In case they were needed, Bailey selected RGN fragmentation grenades, currently used by the Russian military.

He also sourced Russian night-vision goggles and two-way handheld radios.

All of these devices were shit in Bailey's opinion, but he had found the best available following the criteria laid down for him. Why he was directed to do this was way above his pay grade.

Lastly, Bailey had been passed down a request from Todd Miller for Russian Tasers. He had found a device recently invented by Oleg Nemtyshkin, now in production. It was unique in that it could fire repeatedly without recharging, unlike those in use by US and British police that could fire only once or three times at best before needing replenishment.

Meanwhile, Dr. Black, known as 'Q' in Langley, and his team was putting the final touches to working prototypes of a gadget he been asked to build. His department was chartered with the development of purpose-built devices for clandestine operations. Todd called him up and requested a meeting in his lab. As usual, Q started talking at high speed about the research and development leading up to the production of his masterpiece but Miller stopped him midstream and asked for a summary of its capabilities in layman terms.

Q looked offended but stated, "this miraculous little box has three functions: first it has to be plugged into an unused Ethernet connection on any server in a network. It will seek out every connected server and transfer all stored data to the IP address of your choice at high speed. Second, it will erase all of that content on the target servers. Third, it will transmit a pulse to every workstation and server in the network, destroying every CPU, graphics processor and memory module. The net effect is recovery of all the data and destruction of the network, the stored data and all connected computers. It's a new generation of beacons we have used in the past that mapped computer networks, transmitted surveillance software and could deploy destructive malware."

"What about backups they probably take?" asked Miller.

"If they take backups online as most people do, the backups will also be wiped. If they take physical backups and store them elsewhere they will of course survive but the network will still be out of action for some time because none of the servers or workstations will be functional," continued Q.

"Can these devices be easily identified as American in origin?" asked Todd.

"Like most devices these days," explained Q, "the components are sourced from various vendors, some American, some Chinese, some Korean... but though I say so myself, the build quality is comparable to Apple so it depends where these devices are being used. In any event, we would not want this technology to fall into the wrong hands. We believe it's unique."

"Point taken," said Todd, "how quickly can you build four units?"

"Four weeks, possibly less," replied Q.

"Two more questions," said Miller, "how long would a typical download take?"

"Well obviously that's dependent on how much data, but typically a large download might take 20-25 minutes."

"Second question," asked Miller, "if I were using these devices at two separate locations with the same remote servers, and I didn't know which location would connect first, what happens then?"

Q smiled, "we thought of that. The second connection will sense that the remote servers have already been compromised and the device will just download data from the local servers then disable them. Obviously the second operation will run much faster than the first."

Miller thanked him and left.

He returned to his office and called Talbot, asking if he could fly out to Langley ASAP for detailed planning meetings before his team joined them.

"Can you use your own airplane?" Todd asked, "saves the red tape at this end."

"Sure," said Matt, "it's going to cost you a round trip though."

"I'll have my secretary book you a room at the local Hyatt. We'll meet there instead of at HQ. I have a secure meeting room ready with video conferencing equipment in case we need it," said Miller.

It took Matt under two hours to get in the air. His bags had already been packed. He had called his pilot to file a flight plan and have the Learjet fueled and stocked with food and drinks. Federica gave him a ride to Montgomery Field in her Lotus and the airplane left soon afterward. Matt was hungry. He walked to the galley, such as it was, and found sandwiches and made a cappuccino, then lit a cigar and watched the news. A car was waiting for him at Langley airfield and drove him directly to the Grand Hyatt where Todd Miller was waiting. He checked in but asked the bellhop to take his luggage to his room and walked with Todd to the meeting room. Todd, as usual, had arranged for a small buffet, coffee and soft drinks. Matt helped himself to a slice of pizza and salad, passed on the coffee and took just Perrier water.

"Let's start with your ideas for the Shenyang hacker incursions," opened Todd, "beginning with your choice of players. As you can imagine, there's a lot riding on this mission."

"The approach for each of the two locations will differ," started

Matt, "There will be two teams, three people in each, one headed by me, and one by ex-SAS major Smyth. We both speak fluent Russian. Smyth will head up the hotel operation and I'll conduct the incursion into the main hacker location in the Cybertek office block."

"Only three people per team?" asked Miller.

"We have to consider stealth," replied Talbot, "we cannot go in with big teams that would attract unwanted attention. We'll be there as entrepreneurs after all, until the operation starts, after which we need to reassume our declared identities all being well. And I don't believe we'll need more than six people in total to pull this off.

First, the Chilbosan hotel incursion: I took a good look at the hotel before leaving and took a few photographs. The team will check in to rooms previously booked and pay cash in advance for one night. Their baggage must have the appearance of personal effects but will in fact contain their weapons and rappelling gear."

"Rappelling gear?" asked Miller.

"Yes," said Talbot, "I'll get to that. After checking in separately they will take the staircase and meet on the roof of the hotel after dark. They'll have their bags with them. The hotel has sixteen floors and the offices are on the third floor. They'll rappel from the roof and use glass cutters and suction pads to enter the offices through the windows. They will need to have gas masks. If there are any late workers or guards, they'll use CS gas or Tasers to disable them before starting work. They will connect the black box you are supplying, wait until it completes its job, remove it and take it with them. They will exit the same way as they came, climbing back up to the roof, packing their gear and descending the stairs back to their rooms. They will stay the night to avoid suspicion, and then leave the hotel separately with the black box and weapons."

"This sounds far too simple," remarked Todd.

"You know the skills of the people involved," said Matt, "I've outlined the operation assuming nothing goes wrong, but we'll be prepared."

"You need to leave at least one weapon behind for the Koreans to find," added Miller.

"My apologies," said Talbot, "yes, we'll leave a Russian handgun behind."

"I sent you a list of the weapons we have for you," said Miller, "anything missing?"

Without hesitation, Talbot replied, "we'll need knives, equivalent to the American Ka-Bar, and CS gas and masks. We need climbing ropes. We don't need the two-way radios but we do need burner phones with Bluetooth earpieces. We don't need machine guns, but we do need silencers for the handguns."

"Why no machine guns?" asked Miller, "You never know. What's your point?"

"My point is, there is no point. If we have to resort to using them, we've already failed," retorted Talbot.

"OK," replied Miller, "I'll get the armorer working on CS gas, masks, silencers and knives. I'll have Lee go shopping locally for luggage, ropes and climbing gear, surgical gloves and burner phones."

Matt interrupted, "and leather gloves."

"Leather gloves?" asked Todd.

"For abseiling," said Matt.

Todd continued, "I'll also have Lee buy local clothes for everyone. The weapons will be shipped via diplomatic bag to the American Consulate, and we'll include ski masks with labels removed, assuming these will not be available locally. We'll sort out later how we get the bags and their contents to you. No one must wear anything that could be traced back to their countries of origin, no watches, nothing whatsoever. Now how about the office block?"

"A totally different approach," said Talbot, "the block has a 24x7 concierge sitting behind a desk overlooking the entrance from the street. I need your help in obtaining a pass card for one of the other companies in the building, to provide access after-hours. The street entrance has a magnetic stripe card reader. After I gain entrance alone, I'll greet the concierge, Taser him, tie him up and hide him somewhere, then let in the other two team members with our weapons and the black box. We'll lock the entrance door. I'll need access to that drug you use to give the concierge temporary amnesia so he never remembers my face, or anything else about the incident for that matter."

"OK," said Miller, "I'll get Lee working on a pass card, and talk to the armorer about the drug."

Talbot continued, "we'll take the elevator up to the ninth floor, donning our ski masks on the way. We will not enter the suite through the main entrance that has security cameras, but will use another of many entrances that are usually kept locked. We'll pick the lock. If alarms sound we'll disarm them and as with the other operation, we'll enter the offices and use CS gas if there are people present. We'll attach and activate the black box and wait until it's completed its job, then leave the way we came in, leaving one of our handguns. On exiting the office suite we'll destroy the security cameras and their recorders in the entrance lobby since they have my facial features there. When we reach the foyer I'll free the concierge and prop him up behind his desk. When he wakes he will just think he fell asleep."

"Again, it sounds very simple," stated Miller, "but sound. Let's hope nothing goes awry. We'll have to figure out how we get those bags back to Lee who can arrange for most of their contents to be shipped home by diplomatic bag. What happens after that?"

"We all assume our original personas back in our original hotels, using our own clothes and identities. We leave on different flights to Seoul, where we meet up for some kind of celebration."

"I promise to be there for that!" said Miller, smiling.

Miller knew Talbot of old, and while he was over-simplifying a very complex operation, his mind would be working overtime figuring out contingency plans should anything go ass over tit.

"I need to make a call to Nick Bailey the armorer about the additional requirements, and also to Lee in Shenyang," said Todd, "do you need to freshen up before dinner?"

"Good idea," Matt replied, "I didn't even unpack yet."

Matt left the meeting room and returned a few minutes later.

"What do you feel like eating?" asked Todd, "there is a great selection of restaurants right here in the hotel. They even have a Morton's Steakhouse."

"If it's OK with you, Todd, I feel like fish tonight," Matt said.

"Fish it is then; they have an excellent grill also," Todd smiled.

He called the restaurant to make sure they had a table and they left the room.

After they were seated, Todd asked when Matt could fly in his team for a detailed briefing. "We could speed things up if you arrange for a Gulfstream to collect them," said Matt. Todd agreed to make the arrangements in the morning.

No more business that evening since they were in a public restaurant. Matt told Todd about Federica moving in. Wendy was recovering slowly from her emotional crisis but Todd was still in her bad books while running around the world with no respite in sight. He thought his marriage was going down the crapper but didn't share that with Matt. They talked about cars, something else they had in common. Todd lusted after the Jaguar F-Type but on his CIA salary that was unlikely to happen. They left the restaurant but before parting company Todd mentioned he had received a call from Director Peel who had heard from the Secretary of State about the revised plan for destruction of the tunnel. He was very concerned about leaving the laborers down there after we cut off the air and electric feeds.

"What does he want us to do?" asked Matt.

"Rescue them," replied Todd.

"Not a good idea," said Matt, "we would have to drill another tunnel, send people down there to extricate them, and then we have the sarin gas cylinders to worry about."

"What would you suggest?" asked Todd.

"We would learn nothing by rescuing the laborers," said Matt, "we already have a narrow observation shaft reaching into the roof of the tunnel. We extract our fiber-optic cable and thread a flexible pipe in its place, then gas the remaining guys humanely and seal the shaft."

"Sounds awful," said Todd, "but better than leaving them to a slow painful death. I'll suggest that to the Director."

Matt finally reached his room to rest but first called Federica, who was installing her extensive wardrobe in Matt's closets. No travel on the horizon for her but she sounded happy. Matt poured a scotch, turned on the TV but only looked at the pictures, as he frequently had in the past, alone in a hotel bed and forced to listen to a couple making love next door. He slept and not for the first time, questioned what he was doing with his life.

The next morning he visited Spook Central at Todd's invitation.

"Since you're at a loose end until your team arrives, I thought you might be interested in seeing part of our control center," said Todd, as he led the way through a maze of corridors with multiple checkpoints and doors with privileged access rights.

When they arrived at their destination, Matt thought he was in a James Bond movie set. Three of the four walls were bedecked with huge 5K OLED panels displaying real-time views of the trouble spots of the world. Some were updated constantly by unseen servers. Others were monitored and updated manually by operators moving images around on touch-sensitive panels, and calling up new videos as they received instructions over their headsets. There were banks of desks staffed by observers chattering to who-knows-who on their headsets as they monitored activity. Todd walked them to one particular screen.

"As you can imagine, Matt, we need a large fleet of aircraft to be ready to fly at a moment's notice to various parts of the globe and this display shows the types of airplanes, their locations and whether they are en-route somewhere. To get your team members here as quickly as possible we'll likely use two or three planes to collect them and fly them to Langley. I'll be talking to our travel coordinator in a few minutes to get things moving. I just wanted to show you the complexity of what sounds like a simple request," said Todd.

"I'm very impressed," said Matt, "my tax dollars at work."

"What tax?" responded Todd, sarcastically.

Matt ignored that but said, "Actually the travel requirements are simpler than I originally thought they might be. Two of my team are now in the UK, one is in Berlin and two in Paris. One Gulfstream should do it."

He passed Todd a list of names, locations, email addresses and phone numbers. They walked toward the entrance again, and Matt left Todd to his work. He had rented a car and had decided to visit the International Spy Museum in downtown DC.[19] He wasn't expecting much but it should provide a few laughs.

---

19   www.spymuseum.org

Chapter 24
Tunnel Paranoia

Pyongyang and Itaewon, 2017

HYUNG HAD BEEN EXTREMELY irritable these last few days and was increasingly worried about his personal well-being. As the leader of the tunnel project, his progress was under constant scrutiny. The news about the sarin deployment was serious enough to invite even more scrutiny and he was in a foul mood as he joined the latest review meeting. He focused first on KC Park.

"Any word from your mole inside Itaewon?" he asked.

"No sir," Park replied, "he's gone completely silent, which is very uncharacteristic. I made a call to his closest friend in Seoul but he has not seen or heard from Chung at all. He may have been compromised."

The revised plan had been to extend the tunnel to break through into a tributary of the subway system, used for electricity distribution and air-conditioning, then have the sarin cylinders carried to the Itaewon base entrance that would have been opened for them by Chung, the mole.

Hyung turned his attention to BM Min and stated, "We have to assume that Chung is no longer a player and we need a contingency plan. You're going to have to find that entrance from the subway access tunnel, and then cut your way in. You'll need the oxyacetylene equipment."

"That will be almost impossible," said Min, "the equipment is extremely heavy. Our men will be dressed in those ridiculous suits, carrying the sarin cylinders and now the cutting equipment. We will almost certainly be caught."

Hyung's face turned red as he lost his temper, "don't talk to me about problems," he blustered, "talk to me about solutions. We are running out of time. You have five days to devise the new plan."

He stormed out of the meeting room wondering how to explain this latest disaster to his superiors.

Meanwhile, on the Itaewon army base, Chung had been placed under arrest. He had been spotted on security recordings all too often, observing people going in and out of the subway entrance from the base. Having been briefed on the CIA's interest in that entrance, the base commander made a call to the Seoul office that sent over an interrogator following a call to Todd Miller. Chung was not the sharpest tool in the shed and didn't last very long under interrogation. He was a peon, and spouted verbal diarrhea but had nothing of substance to tell. He had been instructed by Pyongyang to observe the comings and goings via the base subway entrance and try to obtain a magnetic access card, a duty he had failed to perform. He was kept under guard on the base until further notice. The privileged subway access door was welded shut, barricaded, and an observation camera monitored 24x7 just in case.

Chapter 25
1600 Pennsylvania Avenue

Washington DC, 2017

PRESIDENT CLINTON HAD called an emergency meeting in the Oval Office after reading the previous two days' briefings. Present were John Peel, Director, CIA; William Mitchell, Secretary of State; Melissa Osbourne, National Security Adviser; General Rushmore, Chairman of Joint Chiefs of Staff; and Bill Patrick, Secretary of Defense.

Clinton first turned to John Peel, requesting a firsthand briefing on the tunnel in Korea.

"Madam President," he started, "we estimate the North Koreans are at least twenty days from reaching Seoul. As I have reported, we have a plan to implode the tunnel as soon as we are given the go-ahead. I am confident we can accomplish that plan given three hours' notice."

"And the North Koreans still know nothing of our discovery of their operation?" asked Clinton.

"No, Madam President, they would have stopped work long ago if they suspected."

"And the Shenyang operation?" asked Clinton.

"The incursion team is flying to Langley from Europe as we speak," replied Peel, "after two or three days they'll be ready to fly to Seoul and onward to Shenyang. Our team leader Matt Talbot is already in Langley with Todd Miller. Everything is under control."

Clinton turned her attention to Melissa Osbourne. The NSA had recently spotted unusual activity from their satellite reconnaissance indicating probable preparations for another missile test. Not only that, but there was activity in North Hamgyong Province, where they had previously conducted underground nuclear tests.

"What in the world do you suppose they're up to now?" asked Clinton.

"As you know, Madam President," she replied shifting uncomfortably in her seat, "they have been unusually quiet since early last year when they exploded their claimed hydrogen bomb.[20] But it seems, after the plethora of sanctions imposed upon them, they have reached breaking point and want to demonstrate their proclaimed strength in as many ways as possible, with simultaneous affronts."

"Exactly the conclusion I have been drawn to myself," acknowledged Clinton, "I wish to take rapid action with several initiatives of our own."

She turned to Mitchell and asked, "please prepare a draft UN resolution to further curb exports of luxury goods of all kinds to North Korea, by that I mean luxury food items, exotic automobiles... in fact anything that Kim Jong-un and his cohorts might normally lust after. The previous resolution does not seem to have been terribly effective. We've long suspected that what little aid they still receive funds the leaders' expensive tastes and does nothing to help the general populace. We may well need another resolution with more punitive measures as we confirm the full extent of our suspicions."

Now Clinton turned to Bill Patrick and the General, and asked, "we talked previously about moving the 7th Fleet off the coast of North Korea. Let's start doing that, but we need something more."

She turned to Mitchell again and instructed him to start making requests to other countries to form a naval coalition to join the 7th Fleet.

---

20   This book was completed in January of 2016, when investigations regarding the strength and type of bomb were still ongoing; there were, however, serious doubts regarding North Korea's claim of possessing a hydrogen bomb.

"I suggest you start with China, who were particularly upset by previous nuclear tests, the UK, the Western European countries who care to join and certainly Russia and Japan, who were also involved in the six-party talks that stopped in 2009. I'll speak personally to Park Geun-hye in Seoul. Of course, we'll need the blessings of Congress but given the mound of evidence we have accumulated I'm not expecting much resistance. I thank you all for that. These are frightening times."

Clinton turned to Bill Patrick again and asked, "If they do indeed launch another missile, can we shoot it down?"

"That would be possible but inadvisable," he said, "they usually conduct their tests over the Sea of Japan and we'd be in political hot water if we took down a missile over those waters."

"Could we do it covertly, from one of the X-37B shuttles you have circling the globe?" she asked.

"It's possible," Patrick replied, "I'll look into it."

"Any other input?" asked the president.

Melissa Osbourne spoke up, "we could consider deploying so-called honeypot servers," she said.

"Please explain," said Clinton.

Melissa continued, "we have employed this technique on a small scale in the past. It involves setting up dummy servers that are difficult to hack into, but not as difficult as our real servers. We could deploy them, for instance, for the NSA, the CIA, Homeland Security; the intention being to feed disinformation. Such information would never be accessible to the public who make simple inquiries; only to those privy to secure parts of the websites. Given prior experience, some governments have succeeded in gaining such access. We would make it easier for them to access these honeypots. And even if they gained access to both the honeypots and the real servers, which should they believe? For our staff without the appropriate high-level security clearances, they will never know of the existence of the honeypot servers and never see the disinformation."

"And you know this could be accomplished?" asked the president.

"Yes, Madam President," replied Osbourne, "we have been looking into it for some time now."

"How long would it take to implement?" asked Clinton.

"About six months," she responded, "but if indeed the Korean hacker network is shut down, it would take much longer than that for them to rebuild it."

"I love it," responded Clinton, smiling, "please put a plan together for my review."

To close the meeting, President Clinton said, "I want a coordinated response; the tunnel closure, the hackers put out of action, the show of force from a naval coalition, the sanctions and the destruction of the missile. We need to hit them everywhere it hurts, including the longer-term honeypot idea. The gloves are off. It's our turn to dial up the rhetoric. Thank you all."

She ordered coffee but then poured herself a scotch instead.

"What a mess, she thought, after just one year in office."

She poured another drink, canceled her remaining appointments for the day, and then left for her private quarters to think this though, determined to make this part of her legacy for the first term. She also wanted to meet this Talbot guy. He had been so successful in Abbottābad, now here he was again. She hoped he would excel himself again in Shenyang.

Soon after the Oval Office meeting, Bill Patrick visited Melissa Osbourne's office and expressed his gratitude for the honeypot server idea.

"It was very brave of you to propose such a plan in its early stages," he said, "do let me know if my people can help in any way."

"Thank you, Patrick," she responded, "I think they can, with your collective wealth of experience in the Pentagon."

He smiled, invited her for a drink, and they left the building.

Chapter 26
The Team Flies In

Langley, Virginia, 2017

AS PROMISED, TODD MILLER made arrangements for a Gulfstream to collect Matt's team. As luck would have it, they had an airplane in Rome, destined to fly back to Langley empty. It was rerouted to Paris Le Bourget airfield, Berlin Schönefeld, and RAF Northolt, after filing flight plans, loading up with fuel, food and drinks, and making calls to the team members.[21] They were a motley crew, dressed in whatever they stood in, with little in the way of carry-on baggage. They would need to go shopping after landing. But they were all on time for their pickups. With the exception of Major Smyth, the newcomer, they all knew each other, having been together during the Abbottābad operation. The pilot, as he had been instructed, announced that the on-board phones, Wi-Fi and other electronic wizardry were out of bounds for security reasons. Other than Smyth and Brennan, none of them had ever taken a flight on a private jet and quickly got into party mood, drinking and smoking up a storm. The two ex-SAS guys conferred and it was Brennan who called a halt and reminded everyone that they had some serious work to do after landing. In any event, the bar was almost dry. Before landing in Langley the flight attendant brought them all large strong coffees.

Talbot and Miller met the airplane when it landed and immediately suggested they book into their rooms at the Hyatt, shower

---

21 RAF Northolt: Increasingly open to private jets; previously restricted to the RAF and Royalty.

and change and join them in the meeting room. Two Ford sedans were waiting to drive them to the hotel. When they reconvened Matt chaired the meeting, explaining what they had to accomplish in Shenyang, and the formation of the teams. The team that Matt himself was to head would include Peter Brennan and Ganja while Smyth's team would be completed by Bang Bang and Lloyd Morris. Todd Miller would also be in Shenyang as a contact point but would not take part in the operation. Between them, Matt and Todd explained the incursion plans for the respective buildings, emphasizing the need to avoid the use of firearms if possible. This was supposed to be a covert operation in the truest sense of the term. The next day would be spent in the CIA HQ, where they would familiarize themselves with the Russian weaponry and Q's gadgets. The day after that they would all fly together on a Gulfstream to Seoul before taking separate commercial flights to Shenyang. For now, they would meet in half an hour to eat in one of the hotel restaurants with strict instructions not to talk about the forthcoming operation.

The next morning they were all escorted to the CIA firing range where Nick Bailey explained their Russian weapons to them and invited them for target practice. As had been expected they all, down to a man, bitched and moaned about the weapons, but their complaints fell on deaf ears. They all became reasonably proficient shots after all said and done.

Then it was time to meet Q. They were escorted to a meeting room. Q had been told to talk in layman's terms about his latest invention that he had dubbed 'Snoopy.' As opposed to the first generation of the device, it was extraordinarily simple to operate and the presentation did not take long.

Todd intervened to make a statement, "these devices must never fall into anyone's hands outside of you, the incursion teams. The intention is for you to carry them out and we'll make arrangements to return them to the US, but if that plan is ever at risk, they must be destroyed."

Then it was Matt's turn, "You'll all have burner phones but they are not to be used except in cases of dire emergency. The only exception to that is when either of the teams completes their mission and gets ready to leave the building, there will be a simple call, in Russian, from one team leader to the other to signal that. It will be a simple 'ya zakonchil,' meaning, 'I'm done,' and the response will be 'yes,' da, Mark?"

"Da," Mark responded.

"Any questions?" asked Todd.

There were none. They returned to the Hyatt to eat and sleep.

The teams were collected the next morning and driven to Langley Airfield where a Gulfstream was waiting. Todd Miller was already onboard. As soon as everyone was seated, they taxied and lifted off. Compared to the previous flight the mood was rather subdued, and not a drop of alcohol was consumed. The long flight to Seoul necessitated two fueling stops when they briefly deplaned just to stretch their legs. They landed at Seongnam Air Base, just south of Seoul, in darkness, and were met and driven to the Millennium Seoul Hilton. They were given instructions to go shopping at first light for smart casual clothes and other necessities and hand over the clothes they were wearing and other possessions, to be returned to them after the operation had been completed. That done, they were issued with their Korean Air return tickets to Shenyang, hotel reservations, business cards and false credentials, credit cards and cash. No more than two of them had been booked on a given flight. Aside from a couple of flight delays, they all reached Shenyang without incident, though both Bang Bang and Ganja, traveling separately, were grilled by Chinese immigration officials, apparently because they simply didn't look like businessmen. How perceptive of the immigration guys! But they were allowed to pass. The team members took taxis to their respective hotels, where each of them had messages waiting at check-in, requesting one-on-one meetings at various tea shops or restaurants the following day. Each message was from a different guy, but following their briefing they knew the meeting was to be with CS Lee from the local CIA office. They had committed his photograph to memory.

The team took taxis the next morning to their brief meetings with Lee where each received a small travel bag. They exchanged small talk for a few minutes then returned to their hotels. Lee had been diligent. Each of the bags was slightly different, but the contents of each one was identical; their weapons and other equipment, some locally acquired and some flown in by diplomatic bag, clothing for the incursions and burner phones. Lee even had the foresight to include field dressings in case they were needed. The bags for Talbot and Smyth also contained their Snoopy devices. They were ready, but it was a waiting game until Talbot gave the 'go' signal. Talbot, in turn, was waiting to hear from Todd Miller who awaited the green light from his boss Director Peel.

Meanwhile, a techie had flown in from the Seoul office to ensure the servers in the Shenyang office were ready to receive transmissions from the Snoopy devices, in preparation for uploading to Langley using their high-speed link.

Chapter 27
The Pieces Come Together

Washington DC, 2017

CONGRESS HAD GIVEN their approval for the actions proposed at President Clinton's recent meeting in the Oval Office. Resistance had been minimal.

Drilling equipment and explosives had been positioned at each of the observation sites above the North Korean tunnel, in South Korea. The specialist teams were waiting for their instructions to go from Dirk Potter, after his call from Director Peel.

William Mitchell made a convincing presentation to the UN Security Council with video evidence of the tunnel digging, and he included detailed shots of the sarin gas cylinders and the handling precautions being taken. The presentation continued with satellite footage taken over the suspected sites for forthcoming missile and nuclear tests. Mitchell concluded his pitch with the plan for destruction of the tunnel but made no mention of the Shenyang hacker operation or the planned downing of the Korean missile by the X-37B. Those actions would be kept under wraps for years to come. Two UN resolutions were passed with little fanfare. The first was to further curtail the export of luxury goods of all kinds to North Korea, as first proposed by President Clinton. The impact on the exporters would be minimal since consumption by North Korea was restricted to a privileged few. The second resolution was for the coalition of naval forces for a massive show of force to demonstrate a united front to the Hermit Kingdom. Responses to the coalition pleas were overwhelming with agreements by the UK, France, and China to join South Korea and the US, with Japan providing logistical support. The Russian navy had been in serious decline after the dissolution of the Soviet Union and though they were rebuilding their capabilities at a furious rate, they had no appropriate vessels within easy reach of North Korea. President Clinton received an apologetic call with an assurance that the US intentions had the full support of Russia. The navies would begin moving their fleets immediately but at the request of Mitchell the resolutions would not be announced until the tunnel actions were in process. Admiral George Pennington of the US Navy was to be in command of the coalition fleet.

Bill Patrick had positioned the X-37B shuttle in range of the Sea of Japan. Its attack capabilities had never been communicated to any other military forces or intelligence agencies, let alone the public at large. It was watching for a North Korean missile launch and communicating constantly via satellite link to the Pentagon. Meanwhile the NSA in Fort Meade, Maryland was continuing to monitor ground activity via satellite.

The United States was almost ready for its multi-pronged response.

Chapter 28
Readying the Offensive

Pyongyang, 2017

JW Hyung was very subdued for a change. The tunnel project was wearing him down, after so many glitches along the way. He turned to BM Min for a status update.

He got straight to the point, "how long now before we can break through into the subway system?" he asked.

"Ten days," replied Min.

"Are the hazmat suits and other equipment ready for the army base incursion?" asked Hyung.

"Yes, sir, everything is ready now," replied Min, wearing one of his rare smiles.

"Let me know immediately if there are any unexpected problems," said Hyung, and closed the meeting.

Meanwhile, in Musadan-ri in North Korea the latest generation of the Taepodong-2 missile was being prepared for launch. The last attempt had been in 2006, and failed in midair after about 42 seconds of flight, falling harmlessly into the Sea of Japan. Extensive improvements had been made over the last few years and the team was confident of a successful test this time around. The theoretical range of the missile was often estimated to be adequate to reach Alaska but analysts in South Korea calculated shorter capabilities that, as far as US interests were concerned, meant the missile could only reach Guam or possibly the sparsely inhabited western tip of the Aleutian Islands. The missile was ready and its launch would be timed to coincide with the tunnel break-through.

Preparations were under way in Punggye-ri for a further underground nuclear test. Previous tests had been undertaken in 2006, 2009, 2013, and early in 2016 after an additional test tunnel had been dug. After the failure of the 2016 test, despite North Korea's claims to the contrary, a new tunnel was immediately started. This new test was also to coincide with the Seoul tunnel break-through.

Chapter 29
Final Preparations for the Response

Various locations, 2017

THE HACKER TEAM IN Shenyang and the tunnel destruction team in Seoul were patiently awaiting the word to move forward. The X-37B shuttle, the Pentagon and the NSA teams were watching and waiting.

Admiral George Pennington was busy planning the biggest war games since Valiant Shield in 2006, when 22,000 personnel, 280 aircraft and thirty ships, including the supercarriers USS Kitty Hawk, USS Abraham Lincoln and USS Ronald Reagan had taken part. At the time, it was the largest military exercise to be conducted by the United States since the Vietnam War. It marked the first of what became biennial exercises involving different branches of the US military. This show of force, accentuated by the coalition, was to exceed the scope of Valiant Shield by far. Permission had been granted by China, Russia and Japan for the combined force to sail by their waters without interference to allow the vessels to stand off both sides of the Korean Peninsula.

The admiral held a video-conference with the commanders of the coalition fleets, many of whom were still en-route, to summarize what they might expect as they conducted their exercise. Participants included the Royal Navy who had two Type 45 destroyers with Sea Viper antiaircraft and antimissile weapons and were currently visiting Singapore. They set sail for Korea immediately. The

French navy had a presence in Papeete, Tahiti consisting of their aircraft carrier Charles de Gaulle, and two light corvettes, ideal escort vessels for an oceangoing task force. They also left for Korea as soon as they could take on supplies for the journey. The People's Liberation Army Navy (PLAN) of China had modern Lanzhou and Luhai-class destroyers with long-range air-defense and supersonic anti-ship missiles, and advanced nuclear-powered attack and ballistic missile submarines close by; those would be the first to reach the 7th Fleet and the South Korean navies. South Korea was ready to dispatch their Harbin and Zhuhai Luha-class guided missile destroyers from the Busan Naval Base. The 7th Fleet itself, other than the vessels already in South Korea, was speeding toward the peninsula from Yokosuka in Japan. Some steamed faster than others given their destination of the west coast of North Korea. For those destined for the east coast, it was a shorter journey across the Sea of Japan. Many of the ships were equipped with the very latest Aegis Combat System, as were some of the ROK vessels.[22] They would flank the country and others joining would be divided between the two coasts.

Admiral Pennington began, "you have all been briefed about the objectives of this exercise already. We need to demonstrate to North Korea the strengths of our respective forces, and perhaps more important that we stand together and will not tolerate their rhetoric and aggression any longer. Our primary objective is one of intimidation. Should they show such aggression in the future they stand no chance against our combined resources. But none of our ships or aircraft must ever enter their territorial waters. We have no desire to provoke them further or contravene international law.

Reports of the strength of the KPN vary, but we do know they are strictly a 'brown water' navy, and never stray beyond their waters.[23] The last reported strength is 60,000 personnel, 708 vessels including 3 frigates and 70 submarines and they operate mainly within the 50km exclusion zone. Their east and west coast

---

22   Aegis: Computer and radar technology to track and guide weapons. ROK: Republic of Korea.
23   KPN: Korean People's Navy.

squadrons cannot support each other given the limited range of most vessels, and that would require circumnavigation of the south of the peninsula. Even in peacetime it's almost impossible for a ship on one side to visit the other coast. The HQ of the East Coast fleet is Toejo Dong, with major bases at Najin and Wonsan. The West Coast HQ is Nampo, with major bases at Pipagot and Sagon Ni. They have a large number of fast patrol craft and guided missile and torpedo boats, policing DPRK territorial waters. Their missiles have radar and infrared heat-seeking capabilities, and they carry 25-37mm guns. Their submarines consist of 4 Soviet Whiskey-class, 22 Chinese ROMEO-class, and an unknown number of DPRK ROMEO-class vessels. Much of the fleet is midget submarines designed to sneak up on South Korean targets. If we have anything to fear, from overzealous North Korean military or stupid orders, it would probably be from the fast patrol, missile or torpedo boats. We must be vigilant and maintain electronic surveillance at all times. Should you detect suspected attacks at any time, contact me immediately. We will not move to international waters off the north of the peninsula until we receive notification that a press release outlining the approved resolution by the UN National Security Council has been issued. Any questions?"

There were none.

In addition, acting on instructions from the Pentagon, two nuclear-capable B-2 stealth bombers were flying directly from Whiteman Air Force base in Missouri; a 13,000 mile round trip with the aid of inflight refueling. As they did in 2013, as part of the annual ROK-US military exercises, they would drop dummy ordnance on the South Korean Jik Do target range.

Chapter 30
Shock and Awe

Various Locations, 2017

PREPARATIONS WERE COMPLETE. Calling from the Situation Room in the White House, President Clinton set things in motion. They would monitor most of the initiatives via real-time video links.

William Mitchell requested the Secretary General of the United Nations to issue press releases announcing the two newest resolutions directed at North Korea. It would be just a matter of minutes before the news reached Pyongyang. This was the trigger to start the other actions waiting in the wings.

The navy coalition steamed at full speed toward the international waters on both coasts of Northeast Korea.

The first explosive charge in the tunnel was detonated at the closest point to the DMZ. The local team no longer had eyes down there but the implosion of the tunnel was evidenced by acoustic detectors placed close by. Marty Lee, the resident tunnel expert in Seoul, quickly took a look at the other tunnel video and audio monitors that should not have been damaged. As expected, he could see nothing but darkness, but could hear shouts of alarm from the laborers. He gave the signal for the detonation of the other explosives, except for the last monitoring position. Here they released the poisonous gas through the shaft before sealing it.

The hotline connecting North Korea to the South was cut by Pyongyang, and instructions were immediately issued to Musadan-ri to launch the Taepodong-2 missile, following which a directive was issued to Punggye-ri to hasten the detonation of the underground nuclear test charge.

As soon as the missile launch was detected by the NSA satellite transmitting to Fort Meade, the Pentagon was notified and instructions were transmitted to the ever-listening X-37B shuttle lurking over the Sea of Japan. The shuttle released its own missile payload; the first live test of its capabilities. Its trajectory had been carefully plotted to ensure no debris rained down on the coalition force below. The missile carried no warhead; its impact with the Korean rocket and its unburned fuel would be adequate. The little missile took only minutes to enter the earth's atmosphere and locate its mark using heat sensors. The results were devastating, but it would appear to those who would later analyze the incident that yet another failure had occurred. No one, except for the few in the know, would ever understand what had really happened.

There were no lingering doubts, however, when seismic activity was detected by South Korea and Japan, closely followed by the Russian Defense Ministry, the United States Geological Survey and the China Earthquake Networks Center. In the Chinese prefecture of Yanbian, bordering North Korea, the impact was so severe that children were sent home from school. A nuclear explosion had taken place inside North Korea at their test site, in total defiance of the CTBT, banning all nuclear explosions everywhere, including underground.[24] Notably, North Korea had never signed the treaty; neither had India or Pakistan for that matter. The yield of the explosion was estimated to be about 10 kilotons, small in comparison with the fission bombs dropped on Hiroshima and Nagasaki yielding 16 and 21 kilotons respectively. Subsequent analysis would show that, following the path of the January 2016 test, this was not a hydrogen bomb, but another fission experiment. Japan immediately summoned an emergency United Nations meeting.

The coalition naval vessels were in position, and began their exercise. It was fascinating to the French, Chinese and Royal

---

24 CTBT: Comprehensive Test Ban Treaty of 1966.

Navy forces to witness firsthand the tactics employed by their US allies. No surprises to the ROK navy who had been here before. It was not long before radar detected small fast boats approaching from both the east and west coasts. Little Birds were immediately launched to reconnoiter and spotted North Korean fast torpedo and missile boats as Admiral Pennington had speculated.[25]

The lead Little Bird pilot radioed his captain to report his sightings and expressed his amazement at their daring, "these guys must be on a suicide mission to go up against such massive forces. Are they insane?"

"Fly back to the carrier," was the response he got, "we'll take it from here."

Radars continued to track the fast-approaching boats and when they were close to crossing into international waters, an extremely loud warning was broadcast in English and Korean, "you are approaching international waters. Turn around or you will fired upon."

They kept on coming. Admiral Pennington did not hesitate and ordered warning shots to be fired. Every class of US Navy surface combat ships carried Phalanx CIWS radar-guided 20mm Gatling guns mounted on swiveling bases.[26] They are formidable counters to anti-ship weapons, firing autonomously once activated at 4,500 rounds per minute. Shots were fired across the bows of each boat, and the verbal warnings repeated. The boats turned around and headed back to the coast except for one that just kept on coming. It was too close for comfort.

"Sink it," instructed the admiral.

The guns poured lead into that boat for just one minute and it was history. Admiral Pennington immediately called the Pentagon to report the incident though they had already watched it play out, real-time, as had the tense audience in the White House Situation Room. The exercise continued unabated.

Over in Shenyang the order to go had been received by Matt

---

25 The MH-6 Little Birds, traditionally used by the US Army for special operations, had been deployed as recon helicopters given their agility.
26 CIWS: Close-In Weapon System.

Talbot and he relayed this to his team by prearranged innocuous text messages to their burner phones.

Smyth, Bang Bang and Lloyd Morris checked into the hotel as planned and made their way to the roof using the elevator as far as they could, then took the staircase. Lloyd was the first one to arrive and he picked the lock leading to the flat roof after checking for alarms. They made their way to the edge where they would need to descend and secured their ropes to hooks, presumably used by window cleaners. They didn't look as if they were used very often but were sturdy enough. They would rappel separately, but first looked over the edge to make sure they descended between the hotel room windows where they would not be spotted. They had changed their plan slightly after discussing with Talbot. Assuming all went well, they would not return this way but would exit to the corridor and take the elevators back to their rooms and wait until the morning. Climbing back to the roof would have taken far too long. They donned their leather gloves, strapped their bags to their backs, and descended cautiously. Fortunately there was little moonlight, thanks to the smog. It was highly unlikely that they would be spotted from below. Thanks to Talbot's photographs they knew there were ledges above and below each window, and they counted their way down until they were just above the third floor. Now came the tricky part. They had to swing over to the ledge above the third floor window using the ledge below the fourth floor to hide their ropes from anyone who might be looking out into the gloom. Smyth used a small mirror to peek through the window. He could have used a fiber-optic gizmo but Talbot had nixed that idea, not wanting to use gadgetry that might give them away if found. All he saw inside were dim lights and three, maybe four nerds still working at their computers with headsets glued to their ears. No sign of guards. He signaled all clear to his colleagues but they waited while Smyth lowered himself farther and began cutting a one-foot diameter hole in the window pane with his glass cutter. He managed to do that without causing a screeching noise as he etched the glass, then used his suction pad to remove it before reaching inside to unlatch the window. He threw CS gas canisters toward the workaholics after donning his gas mask, and then unlatched the other windows for his partners. They exchanged their leather gloves for surgical ones and got to work, looking for the main server. Smyth attached his Snoopy device and they waited for it to perform its magic, while making sure the Koreans were at least comfortable while they had tears still streaming from their eyes as they coughed uncontrollably. It was all over in less than thirty minutes when Snoopy signaled it was done with snooping and destroying. They discovered that the video monitors in the lobby recorded their images on one of the local servers also and those records has been erased as part of the operation, as were those at the Pyongyang end, but the risk of physical backups in North Korea remained and there was sod-all they could do about that. They removed their gas masks and placed everything in their bags, closing the windows in preparation for their exit. Smyth left his Russian handgun by the side of one of the geeks, and relieved him of his access card. He made the brief 'success' call to Talbot on his burner phone and they left the offices after destroying the surveillance cameras for good measure, taking separate elevators to their rooms. Thanks to Talbot's survey, they did not expect or see any CCTVs. They stayed the rest of the night there though sleep was not forthcoming, but there were no interruptions. They checked out the following morning at staggered intervals and returned to their original hotels.

Meanwhile, the Korean geeks in the offices recovered from the onslaught of the CS gas invaders and one was surprised to see a gun by his side. Then they all saw the opening in one of the windows. Horrified, they discovered that their computers were completely inoperable. Finally, one of them picked up his cell phone and called Choe, the GM, who immediately called Pyongyang then the local police. When the police arrived they were mystified. No fingerprints anywhere and no immediate evidence of serious damage or theft, just a window pane that had been broken into from the outside and the wrecked cameras. They saw the abandoned ropes dangling outside the windows and took them as evidence. They also took the handgun, later discovered to be of Russian origin. None of the Korean geeks had been harmed; in fact the invaders had gone to great lengths to ensure they were comfortable while suffering from the effects of CS gas, also Russian in origin.

    Talbot had been simultaneously tackling the main office building with Peter Brennan and Ganja. Using his access card, Talbot entered the lobby alone while his partners hid themselves outside the entrance. He approached the attendant behind his desk and asked to check the sign-in book on the pretext of checking whether colleagues were in the building. As he got closer he Tasered the guy, then injected him with the amnesia-inducing drug and lowered him to floor, securing him with cable ties out of sight of the entrance. He unlocked the entrance again to let in his partners and relieved Ganja of his bag as they walked toward the elevator. The corridor outside the Cybertek offices was dimly lit as they sought out one of the unused access doors. They wore their gas masks as Ganja picked the lock. They were in but not before an alarm sounded. Brennan quickly silenced it but the damage had been done and an armed guard appeared out of nowhere to investigate. Talbot slammed his fist into his jaw and lowered the unconscious guy to the floor. They looked around briefly and it was a proctologist's dream; wall-to-wall assholes, including another two guards and ten nerds immersed in their work. The invaders quickly threw CS gas canisters and waited for them to do their work. Unfortunately one of the guards started firing his gun blindly, and an unlucky shot caught Ganja in his right arm. It started bleeding profusely but Talbot rushed over as Brennan disarmed the guards before securing them with cable ties. Talbot found a field dressing and applied it as best he could to Ganja's wound to quench the blood after removing his jacket, and gave him a mild pain killer. They started exploring and after locating the main server, found an unused Ethernet port and woke Snoopy to put him to work. Talbot noticed that most PCs were still using Windows XP, now all of seventeen years old; others were using an unrecognizable operating system. During analysis of the code, Langley later discovered this was North Korea's homegrown Red Star OS3.[27] Matt returned to Ganja to make sure no blood was seeping out. They wanted no telltale DNA left behind. Snoopy blinked a light to signal he was finished and Talbot returned him to his bag, then walked over to Ganja again and asked him in Russian if he could walk after his sedative. He grunted an affirmative, stood shakily, replaced his jacket, and the small group made for the door. Talbot hesitated then walked back to leave his gun. He had almost forgotten in the heat of the moment. Brennan picked up Ganja's bag and they made their way back to the office block foyer after destroying the surveillance cameras. Talbot removed the guard's cable ties and the Taser prongs and propped him up behind his desk. He would soon recover consciousness with no recollection of what had happened. They left the building and Talbot made a brief call to Todd Miller to tell him that the party went well, but one of the guys needed to sober up. Miller immediately recognized the code and told him to use two taxis, one of which was for him to help the drunken soul to his home. He called Director Peel, then CS Lee who would arrange for a doctor to go to the hotel. Fortunately Ganja's wound was mostly superficial; lots of blood but no serious damage, and he was a resilient SOB. After he was patched up, Ganja left Talbot's hotel and returned to his own.

One of the nerds in the Cybertek offices finally had the presence of mind to call Jeong, the GM, who, like his peer before him, called Pyongyang followed by the local police. But once again, the police were mystified. There was no damage or evidence of theft. No one was hurt other than a few bruises to the guards. A Russian gun and empty CS gas canisters were taken as evidence, but evidence of what? When one of the nerds tried to use his computer it was obvious that some real damage had been done, but not something he could share with the police. He did, however, make another call to Jeong.

The next morning Talbot's team went through a set of clandestine meetings similar to the ones when they had collected their

---

27   The Red Star project was initiated by Kim Jong-il. It has the guts of Linux, the look of Mac OS, and spies on its users.

bags from Lee. One by one, they met him in various tea shops or restaurants and handed over the bags. Lee drove the bags back to the US Consulate in two batches. The weapons and Snoopy devices were to be sent back home in the diplomatic bag. Everything else was incinerated. The next day each of the team members started taking separate Korean Air flights back to Seoul. The last to leave was Todd Miller, but not before he had made reservations for the team at the Hyatt hotel, and left instructions for the mother of all parties to be laid on for them.

The mood in the White House Situation Room was ecstatic. They had no eyes on what had transpired in Shenyang but when the call from Director Peel came through all the pieces fell into place. Champagne flowed that evening.

The mood in Pyongyang was rather different. The only action that went off without a hitch was the nuclear test, albeit, once again, with a disappointing yield. They once again announced to the world that they had successfully exploded a hydrogen bomb, but as in 2016 doubts were raised given the detected yield. Their missile had mysteriously exploded before reaching its planned trajectory over the Sea of Japan, after months of exhaustive testing. The tunnel, after huge expenditure and labor, had been destroyed along with the probable deaths of twenty faithful laborers. But perhaps worst of all, mysterious invaders had somehow wrecked the brunt of their hacking operations. It would take several months before they could painstakingly reconstitute the network and all of its hardware. The data they had collected were mostly gone forever, and cyberattacks in the foreseeable future were out of the question.

Matt Talbot and his band of reprobates had arrived in Seoul to a heroes' welcome by carefully selected members of the local CIA and South Korean dignitaries. Two limousines conveyed them to their hotel so they could wash off the Shenyang grime and change into new clothes that were waiting for them. Todd Miller traveled separately to ensure the arrangements were complete before briefly going to his room to compose himself.

A banquet room had been set aside and the food and drinks

just kept on coming. In days of old, kisaeng parlors had been a familiar feature of life in Korea for men looking for relaxation and indulgence of every kind. Those days were mostly long-since gone, but Miller had given instructions to replicate the experience for this evening. Delightful ladies joined those who wanted their company, and the soju flowed while the girls made sure their guests were well fed. Matt excused himself to finally make a call to Federica who answered on his first try and asked when he would be home.

"Very soon now," he replied, "I'll call you from the plane. I look forward to seeing you."

"Me too, darling," she replied, "I have a couple of surprises for you."

Matt returned to the festivities but declined the company of a willing girl. He drank a little and had a quick word with Todd before retiring for the night.

Late the next day the CIA Gulfstream was waiting for them and flew the entire team back to their destinations of choice. A few partied on the airplane but mostly they just slept. After dropping off five of the team at Northolt in the UK, they continued to Langley where Todd and Matt shook hands as they said their goodbyes for now.

Finally, the airplane landed at Montgomery Field close to Matt's home. Federica was there, surprisingly driving Matt's old Ford pickup truck. She drove home recklessly and as soon as they reached their home in La Jolla Farms, Winston came bounding over to greet Matt and almost knocked him over with his enthusiasm.

"Give me a few minutes," said Federica, as she disappeared to the bedroom.

Matt dutifully waited a few minutes before entering. There she was laying on the bed in her birthday suit, surrounded by lighted candles.

"What are trying to do to me?" he asked, "seduce me or set me on fire?"

"A mixture of both," she replied. "I need to take a shower," said Matt, staring at her exquisite form.

"Be quick," she said, "or I'll have to start without you."

It was quick, very quick.

After they relaxed a little, Matt asked, "so what was the other surprise?"

"You'll just have to wait until the morning," she said.

They slept at peace with the world.

Epilogue

THE MORNING AFTER MATT'S RETURN home, Federica led him to the garage and turned on the lights. There, sandwiched between his Bentley and Aston was a gleaming Ferrari-red LaFerrari.

"Holy shit!" were the only words that came out of Matt's mouth at first, "did you win the lottery?"

"No," she said, "I earned a nice bonus in Vienna, I rented out my townhouse and sold the Lotus, and then I bought the new car for a song from a guy who recently declared bankruptcy. Shall we go out for lunch? You can drive but if you bend it I'll cut your nuts off."

"You wouldn't like that," he said chuckling as he fired up the 949hp Italian powerhouse.

He smiled all the way to one their favorite lunchtime haunts. Coincidentally, Captain Brian Philips and his wife were drawing into the parking lot just as Matt screeched into his space. Brian smiled as they emerged from the car and just wagged his finger. It was good to be home again, and just in time for Christmas.

Todd Miller returned home to a different kind of surprise. His wife was filing for divorce. He had half expected it, but was still in a state of shock for the next few days. The only good to come out of the mess was when Wendy bought him out of the house and he was able to buy a smaller property and an (almost) new F-Type Jaguar. As for marriage, he was still wedded to his job.

Following a recommendation by Todd Miller endorsed indirectly by Matt Talbot, CS Lee was promoted to a new assignment as head of station in Singapore. It was a city he loved and was massively relieved to kiss goodbye to Shenyang.

Matt received a surprise phone call from CIA Director Peel who, after thanking him for his exemplary performance in the Korean affair, offered him a job. Matt was taken aback at first, but out of politeness asked for time to think about it, though he already knew his answer would be no. He was not employed full-time by any means, but his fees already exceeded what his salary expectation would be and were tax-free. Why in the world would he want to change that?

President Clinton directed William Mitchell talk to South Korea and Japan who both pledged to join in presenting further North Korean sanction recommendations to the UN Security Council. China's help was crucial; they had repeatedly condemned the nuclear tests but were often accused of doing little to stop them. They were rapidly running out of punitive measures, but it was time to call for a complete moratorium on financial aid. It had become abundantly clear that the funds contributed over the years, albeit for increasingly smaller amounts, were never used to help the general populace that had been the intention. Cessation of financial aid would hurt where it mattered, at the top of the regime. The resolution was adopted with no dissension. A further resolution was adopted to step up searches for remnants of sarin gas reserves still held by countries such as Syria. The US had mostly only anecdotal evidence to present since the gas cylinders in the tunnel had been buried, but Mitchell showed videos of the cylinders being moved in the tunnel, supplemented by documents the CIA had obtained pertaining to purchases through agents in Damascus.

Radiation-sniffing WB-135 planes were flown to Korea as they had been following previous nuclear tests, to detect the type of the recent explosion by sampling the atmosphere. Additional military assets were moved to South Korea. The South stepped up its controversial propaganda broadcasts over the DMZ from its huge banks of powerful loudspeakers.

Investigations of the mysterious break-ins in Shenyang continued for a few months, but nothing was ever concluded. It became a very strange cold case. City officials were perplexed when the

Cybertek offices were suddenly shut down, and by the sudden exodus of hundreds of Korean workers. No one enlightened them. Protests were initially made to Russia given the presence of the weapons at the Cybertek sites, resulting in strong denials. The protests were ultimately dropped given the lack of any conclusive evidence.

Stories of the North Korean tunnel and its destruction by South Korean and US forces were the hottest topics in the news media for several weeks. There were no leaks of the demise of workers who died down there. The other hot stories reported were about the newest nuclear test, the failure of yet another missile test over the Sea of Japan, and the foolish attack on an American warship in international waters. North Korea was not winning any popularity contests.

The 7th Fleet and the coalition completed their exercise without further interference. No protests about the loss of the fast torpedo boat and its crew were ever uttered by Pyongyang.

In Pyongyang JW Hyung and his team simply disappeared overnight, and a thorough investigation was initiated in the missile factory where more heads would roll. It would take months to rebuild the cyber-hacking capability, and the loss of data culled over the last few years was devastating. They never did discover how their network was destroyed or by whom though they had their suspicions. Their techies were trying to figure out how to prevent such attacks in the future, while a think-tank had been established to figure out where to locate the team, because Shenyang was now out of the question. Further nuclear tests were put on hold.

The honeypot servers were almost ready to go live after weeks of midnight oil burned by the techies responsible. The US administration was almost ready to spew out disinformation to those who might break through the intensified barriers recently installed. The data extracted from the Korean servers were invaluable, providing a map of what they had seen and what they may have discerned.

❖

The big surprise to Talbot came when he received a call from the White House with an invitation to meet the President. He made hurried plans though had no idea what to expect. He arrived at the appointed time three days later and was escorted to the Oval Office where President Clinton, CIA Director Peel, Bill Patrick, Secretary of Defense, and a photographer were waiting. He was awarded the Presidential Medal of Freedom, the highest award that could ever be bestowed upon a civilian. After photographs had been taken, Peel explained that they were for White House records and his personal memento only. For obvious security reasons, they would never be released elsewhere.

"Thank you for your service, Mr. Talbot," said President Clinton, "you have accomplished a great deal and contributed significantly to curbing the ambitions of a rogue nation."

It was one of those rare occasions when Talbot felt humbled and was grinning like a Cheshire Cat, but said, "thank you, Madam President, I am truly honored."

What no one else in the room understood were his smiles at the memory of words exchanged with Todd Miller when they talked about the analogy with hemorrhoids and assholes. The formalities over, he left with his escort then drove to join Federica at their hotel for a late lunch, wondering why he had not been invited to stay for lunch at the White House. Probably because he had been grinning like a simpleton.

Pyongyang had been uncharacteristically silent since their multiplicity of failures, but suddenly they announced they would like to recommence the Six-Party talks that had collapsed in 2007. The news was welcomed with open arms by the international community, as the Republic of Korea, the Democratic People's Republic of Korea, the United States of America, the People's Republic of China, Japan and the Russian Federation prepared for the first of the new series of meetings. The objectives set forth in agreement with the United Nations Security Council were to have North Korea rejoin the Nuclear Non-Proliferation Treaty, and once again shut down its nuclear facilities and allow nuclear inspectors back into the country. The hope was to return to the point reached back in 2007 and move toward normalization of relations with the United States and Japan in exchange for fuel aid. The newest sanctions, besides those imposed in 2015 blacklisting several foreign agents and trading companies known to help in the proliferation of WMD and conventional weapons, were finally having the desired effect.

President Clinton's job approval rating rose to an all-time high of 74%, topping that of her husband's best score during his second term.

Hassan, now fully recovered from his accident in the UK, had finally been escorted back to Pakistan where he was placed under house arrest. The British and Pakistani governments were still arguing about the bills for his transgressions and hospitalization. His so-called arrest was an oxymoron. He was already making arrangements to change his name again and obtain a new passport to conclude the Talbot business.

Trevor Dodd

Dodd's debut novel, *A Case for Drones*, drew on personal experiences in unsavory parts of the world, including the USSR during the Cold War, Pakistan, and Iran immediately prior to the 1979 ouster of the Shah, and far more pleasurable experiences in such countries as Italy, Sweden, the Hawaiian Islands and Tahiti.

This, the second novel in the Matt Talbot series, draws on personal experiences following several years living in the rural countryside of the UK before moving to London, and numerous visits to South Korea and China beginning in 1979.

A native of England, Dodd is a former executive in the information technology industry, during which he lived in ten countries across the world and visited fifty. He lives in Southern California, where he is at work on his next Matt Talbot story and can be contacted at Trevor's Books.[28] Dodd previously published *Trevor's Travels: Stories of a world traveler in the information technology industry; His adventures, challenges, opportunities, and romances*; available in both kindle and paperback versions, from Amazon.com.